You Are Now Entering Suddence

Emily Welkin Chen

ISBN: 978-1-7383818-0-7

PART I:
Don't Talk to Strangers

THE CASHIER HASN'T called the cops yet. But she will, eventually. No one overlooks a sopping-wet kid all alone in a truck stop diner in the middle of the night.

So I keep her in the corner of my eye while I mow down my fries and watch the cars zip by outside. Sometimes a car pulls in. Most of the times they don't.

One thing they all have in common though: they're all going east to west, the exact opposite of what I want. I just need one single car to be going west to east so it can take me where I need to go.

Assuming the driver will let me hitch.

Which they probably won't.

A car passes. East to west.

I slurp my drink. The ice cubes rattle in the cup.

Another car passes. East to west.

The duct tape on my left shoe slinks to the linoleum. I pick up the slimy mess and slap it back in place.

Another car. East to west.

I wish I had ice cream. But I know for a fact it costs more than the two leftover quarters in my pocket.

Another car. East to west.

The cashier still hasn't reached for the phone. Maybe she knows I'm watching.

Another car.

West to east.

And it pulls into the rest stop.

Dear brand spanking new diary!

Well. You're not new. You got donated to the thrift store because you were all wrinkly and old. I think somebody dropped you in a puddle. You were put in the "free" pile, so I took you. But you're new to me! So that counts for something.

I made three new friends today! Their names are Daniel, Curtis, and Lory, short for Lauren. I see them a lot. I think one of them is the motel owner's kid, so they're always hanging out in the basketball court after school. I've never played with them.

They're teenagers, so I thought they might be mean. Plus, Marisa doesn't let me play in the court unless nobody else is there. But today I was in the parking lot waiting for Marisa (she said there were problems with the credit card machine) and they accidentally threw the ball over the fence and they asked me to give it back to them. I thought about showing off and chucking it right over the fence. They would have been sooooo impressed. But Marisa says I have to be ~inconspicuous~ so I just brought the ball to the door.

Daniel is the one who takes it from me. He has moppy brown hair and a lot of freckles. He's so tall it makes me jealous. He actually recognized me! He asked if I was the kid from 104. I didn't realize he noticed me. Maybe he saw me watching them play through the window. But anyway, at first I was kind of nervous. What if he realizes I'm the kid on TV? Would he tell his parents? And there's that thing Marisa always tells me:

But Daniel just asked me if I wanted to play. He said the other two were "ganging up on him" but then the other two said he was a liar.

I'm supposed to say no. But Marisa was still inside the office trying to get the card to work or something. And Daniel and them looked nice, so I said yes.

He introduced me to Lory and Curtis. Curtis is even taller than Daniel, but he's skinny. Lory looks kind of like Daniel, all freckly with puffy hair. She wears her hat backwards. I'm wearing my hat backwards now because I think it's cool :) She asked if I knew how to play, and I said yes, which felt like a lie even though it wasn't. I DO know how to play. But that doesn't mean I'm any good at it. Especially with dribbling. But I couldn't take it back because I already said it. And I really reeeeaaaallllyyyy wanted to play with them.

Lory said the game ends at 3:00, which was about two minutes away, and me and Daniel were five points behind.

Curtis got the ball first. But then he missed, and I got the rebound. I didn't even try dribbling. I would trip and look stupid. I just threw it at Daniel, but uhhhhh well, SOMETHING happened. I'm not supposed to tell anyone. Not even you, diary. Sorry. But the point is I may or may not have made the ball fly a liiiittle too hard and fast, and Daniel most definitely noticed when he caught it. He was shocked. I could tell. And I felt really bad because I broke one of our cardinal rules: BE NORMAL. But thankfully he cared more about winning than wondering how a 10-year-old with noodle arms could throw like that. He got a three-pointer in. He made it look so easy. The ball didn't even touch the rim. Lory and Curtis were so upset they screamed like cavemen.

SCORE: 30 - 32

By this time there were only twenty seconds left. We HAD to get another three-pointer if we wanted to win. Curtis was mega hogging the ball and faking left and right and trying to trick Daniel. I didn't think Daniel would get tricked since he's the MVP, but he did. Curtis faked going left and threw the ball to Lory. But he didn't trick ME. I went to block the ball. I wanted to catch it, but I just ended up smacking it down the court.

I thought it was over. The ball was going to go out of bounds. I'm not fast enough to catch up to it. But Daniel ran after it for his life. He saved it JUST before it went out, but all he could do was slap it back onto the court because he was running so fast he smashed into the fence. I got the ball in the corner, outside the three-point line, AKA the worst place ever. Five seconds left, so I HAD to shoot. I aimed as well as I could and shot the ball. I closed my eyes because I didn't want to cheat. I wanted to win fair and square. I really, REALLY tried to keep my eyes shut. But then I couldn't help it. I opened my eyes and saw the ball bounce on the rim, doing one of those things where it just bounced and bounced and you couldn't tell if it was going to go in or not.

I probably shouldn't say this. I gave the ball a little nudge. It was such a teeeeeensy itty bitty push. It probably didn't make much of a difference.

Anyway, the ball went in‽‽‽

SCORE: 33 - 32‽‽‽‽‽

Lory picked me up and spun me around so much I thought I might get flung out. All three of them gave me a giant group hug.

Curtis said I should sign the ball so that he can sell it for lots of money when I become a famous player. It was just a joke, but it made my cheeks all hot and itchy and I couldn't stop laughing.

I don't want to make Marisa sound like the bad guy, but when I heard her call my name, it was like everything inside me sank. I didn't want to go. I wanted to hang out with Daniel and Curtis and Lory. But that's a stupid thought, and probably selfish. So I said goodbye and left.

Marisa asked if I won. I said yes. She asked if I cheated. I said no. I'm not supposed to lie to Marisa. But it's just a little lie. I don't think she really cares, anyway. She's only asking to be nice.

I asked if we could get a new basketball. The one I have is something we got from the side of the road at the last motel we were in. It's all gross and leathery and peeling. You can't even see the lines on it anymore. Marisa said "I'll think about it."

And then I told her I wanted to change my name. She said I'm allowed to change my name to anything as long as she can pronounce it. Not ~officially~ of course. I changed it to Dany, like Daniel and Lory mixed together. She said okay! I feel kind of bad for leaving Curtis out. Sorry, Curtis. Maybe you can be our fake last name. Dany Curtis. Marisa Curtis. Sounds good enough.

I wish I had one of those instant cameras so I could take a group picture with them. Marisa wouldn't have let me, so I would've had to take it secretly. I like them a lot. I don't want to forget them. But having their picture might also get them into trouble :'(

Well. At least this will all be over soon! I'm not a good drawer, but this is what they look like.

THE WOMAN FROM THE CAR steps into the diner like she doesn't want to be there. She has long hair and brown skin and a powder-pink denim jacket, the shoulders wet with rainwater. She rubs the soles of her heeled boots on the floor mat, looks around, and sighs. A heavy one.

I get it. There's barely anyone in the diner. Aside from me, there's a silent lumberjack and a half-asleep family and the cashier and the one fry cook in the back. The emptiness is filled with tinny radio music. It's a sad, sad sight.

The woman flicks rainwater from her purse and heads for the booths.

"Excuse me, ma'am," the cashier says. "You have to order."

I can tell the woman wants to sigh again. She manages a sharp inhale, her dark eyes widening like she has to physically restrain them from rolling to the back of her head, before some shred of politeness kicks in and she turns back to the counter with her face schooled back to neutral. She squints at the menu and says, "A hashbrown."

The cashier taps the order in. "Anything else?"

"*No.*"

"That'll be two dollars."

The woman pays with a card and sits in a booth. Right behind me.

I can hear her nails on her phone as she types furiously, and I can hear her swearing under her breath. But when I try to look through the reflection of the window to see what she's typing, all I see is a blurry, bright rectangle.

I look at her car instead. It's an old truck, pink like her jacket and all dirty and scuffed. I could sneak into her trunk while she's busy typing out the world's longest angry text, but what if she turns back west? Then I would be even farther away, and I'd have to make this journey again, and I don't have the time.

The woman's phone vibrates, and she picks up not with a hello, but a hissed, "Aaron, what the *hell?*"

A garbled voice on the other end.

"No, you're going to tell me what's going on right the hell *now*. No—I *told* you, I'm not at my place because they kicked me out—because *you* didn't pay up—"

More garbled reply. I catch a lot of *sorry*'s.

"I need that money *now*. Not next week. *Now*. These two—" She lowers her voice. "These two assholes have been tailing me all day, asking about you, when you're going to pay them back—I don't give a *shit* what their names are. Tell them to back off. Better yet, why don't *you* come *here* so they can stop bugging me—hello? Hello?"

The angry *clat!* of her phone snapping shut. I glance

at the window. In the reflection, the woman has her head in her hands, silently mouthing what must be more swear words. If she's so angry, she definitely won't let me hitch a ride.

So I wait.

I finish the last of my fries.

I stir my ice cubes and slurp up the cold water.

I listen to one, two, three songs about clubbing and one commercial about a nearby bagelry.

Then I make sure the tape is tight on my shoe before hopping out of the booth and facing the woman.

"Hi," I say.

The woman looks up. Her eye makeup is a little smudged. From crying, I guess. She looks left and right as if my parents might be around.

I clear my throat and put on my best smile. "You're heading east, right?"

She scowls. "What?"

"Can you drive me to Ornament County?"

She looks around again. I want to tell her that doing that won't make my parents suddenly appear because they died when I was a baby, but that would ruin the story I worked up.

"My family and I," I explain. "We were on a roadtrip. We got separated. I know how to get home, but I just need someone to drive me there."

She looks around. Again.

Finally, she says, "I think that's something you should tell the police."

"I don't want trouble," I say. "I just want to go home."

"Well, I don't want trouble either." She says it like

it's obvious, which I guess it is. "Look. Go to the nice cashier lady and tell her you're lost."

"But I'm not lost."

She makes a sound of exasperation and looks out the window. Right as a black van pulls in.

Her face drops. "Oh, shit."

Two men get off the van. The woman begins gathering her things.

"Look," she says in a rush. "I'm sorry. I can't help you. I—" She spots the backdoor by the washrooms. "I have to go. Just—just ask the cashier for help, alright?"

Without waiting for an answer, she runs. No, she…flees. That's the word.

I sink back into my booth and stare up at the stained ceiling. Of course it wouldn't be so easy. Now to wait for another west-to-east car. Preferably before the cashier finally gives in and calls the cops.

Indistinct shouting outside. I tilt my head just enough to see the men from the van. They've found the woman's pink car, but the woman isn't there.

Where is she, anyway?

There. Around the corner of the gas station convenience store, keeping tabs on the men. I cup an ear to the window.

"Spread out," Man #1 says. "She has to be here somewhere."

Man #2 heads to the convenience store. Man #1 heads towards the diner.

I pretend I wasn't just eavesdropping on them and poke at my ice cubes with my straw. Man #1 pushes through the glass doors and scans the room like a robot killing machine. He steps up to the counter.

"We're looking for someone." His voice is like a robot killing machine too, deep and steely. "Long hair, Middle Eastern, probably wearing pink."

The cashier slowly looks him up and down, as if searching for a reason to care. "Don't know. Could get my manager."

Man #1's phone rings. He picks it up and listens. Then his eyes go to the convenience store.

"No need," he says to the cashier. "Have a good day."

He marches out. Instead of entering the convenience store, he goes around it. Right to where the woman is hiding.

Oh, this can't be good.

I grab my backpack and hurry after him.

Dear Diary,

Hi again. It's the same day. I just thought you'd like to know what's up.

Marisa's taking me to a ball game today. Usually she would have said this is too "risky" and "we might get caught" but this time, she said it's our only chance to make enough money.

"Enough money for what, Dany?" you might ask, and I'll say "Enough money to leave the country!" I don't know how that works. We might be buying fake passports (!) or maybe even bribing someone (!!!). Usually we make money by picking pockets. Sometimes we raid vending machines. We take all the change too, even though Marisa hates doing that because coins are heavy. But I like it because sometimes I find special coins. I get to keep those.

Anyway, they're both super slow ways of making money. I told Marisa we could rob a bank, or at least an ATM, but she said no. It's a surefire way to attract Them.

The tickets for the game aren't cheap. We don't have that much money to begin with. But Marisa said it's called an investment and we just have to hope that we'll win more money than we paid. Except we don't have to ~hope~ because our team is 100% winning. I've been practicing.

That makes it sound like I'm playing in the game, huh. I'm not. I wish I was. But hey! Once we get the money, we can leave the country, and I can finally go to school for real again and I can join the basketball team and ONE DAY...I'll try out for Real Basketball.

We just found a parking spot. I'll tell you about the game later.

꞉ Halftime break ꞉

So anyway, the reason we're at the basketball game is because we're betting. Before the game, Marisa took me to a casino and did...something. I'm not sure what. I guess this is where you place bets. And THEN we went to the stadium and she got us tickets. Our seats are in the middle and farther from the court than I was imagining, but it's good enough. Except it's pretty crowded, and the guy beside me kept squeezing me. The best thing happened when I finally elbowed him back and he tried to tattle to Marisa, but she just looked at him. You don't want her to look at you like that. It's not good for your health.

⸚Pros and Cons of Being At A Live Game⸚

PROS:
-SO exciting
-I can cheer for real
-Feels like a party

CONS:
-Loud
-Sweaty
-Can't hear a single WORD the
commentators are saying
-So far away from the court

The money‽‽‽ If the team Marisa bet on
wins, then we'll win a ton of money, especially
since we're betting on the "loser team." That's
different from the "losing team," by the way.
Marisa told me the team we bet on almost
never wins, so everybody is betting against
them. Pretty safe bets. Except I'm going to
make sure our loser team wins this time.
    "But how will you do that, Dany?" Well,
diary, I'll tell you a secret.

⩴ I HAVE SUPERPOWERS!!! ⩵

They're called ⩴sparks⩵ and they're
⌐invisible⌐.

But I'm not supposed to tell anyone, okay?
So don't be mad if I have to burn you.

Game over! Marisa in washroom. Short time
to write. Here's what happened.

Points pretty tied for whole game. I didn't
have to do much.

Fourth quarter: our team losing by few
points. 73 to 75. 0.4 seconds left. Marisa kind
of mad I let it get to this point. I think it's
more fun.

Ref blows whistle, ball passed out. They
hurl the ball basically immediately because
no choice. It's not going to make it.

That's when I released my ⩴SPARKS!!!⩵

First one: boost the ball farther.

Second one: push ball down towards hoop.

Third one: little adjustment to the left.

Last one: ball hits the board and spins in
hoop. It's about to fall the wrong way. I make
it fall the right way.

76 to 75!!! We win!!! Marisa hugged me
and said I did a good job_____

I CAN HEAR them shouting before I even reach the alley.

"Give it *back!*" the woman is hollering. "Or I swear to god I'll—"

The jangle of things falling to the ground. I peek around the corner. Man #1 is upending the woman's purse all over the pavement. He picks up a brown wallet and pokes through the pockets.

"No cash in here." He fishes out a crumpled bill. "Except this."

Man #2 shoves the woman into the wall. "Where's the rest of it?"

"I told you, I don't *know*," the woman snaps. "We split up a week ago."

"Do you know where he *might* be?"

"I don't know!"

"Keep it quiet. We don't want to draw attention."

"We?" The woman snarls a laugh. "I didn't realize it was *we*."

"We all hate Aaron here, don't we?" Man #2 plants a hand on the wall, right beside the woman's head. "One last time, Zahira. Where. Is. He?"

The woman—Zahira—gets real close to him. "I. Don't. Know."

"Alright, enough." Man #1 drops the wallet and flicks out a pocket knife. "Talk, or we start—"

"Dude," Man #2 hisses. "Not here."

Man #1 makes a throaty sound. "What are we supposed to do then?"

"We take her hostage. Force Aaron out."

Zahira growls. "Like *hell* you will."

She kicks him in the shin with her heeled boot and runs.

Or tries to. Man #1 catches her around the waist and wrestles her back.

"Let go!" Zahira yells, beating him with fists, elbows, and boots. "Let go or I'll scream!"

"Yeah?" Man #1 says. "We'll be gone by the time the cops get here." He nods to Man #2. "Get her legs."

I step into the alley. "Let her go."

They don't jump like I was hoping they would. But they do look at me with alarm.

"Nothing's happening here, kid," says Man #2, while Man #1 drops Zahira. "Run back to your mom and dad now."

I glance at Zahira. Man #1 has her arm trapped in a tight grip. She's looking at me incredulously at first, and then with a clear warning: *get the hell out of here.*

I don't listen to her.

I step forward and say, as low as I can, "Leave her alone."

"I'm not sure you understand what's happening here,"

Man #2 says. "This is adult business. Run along now."

I don't listen to him either.

I clench my fists, and sparks launch Man #2 into the brick wall. Zahira yelps. Or maybe it's Man #1. I'm not sure, and I don't care. I focus the next spark on the hand gripping Zahira's arm.

Crack!

Man #1 screams, clutching his hand, and then I blast him back one meter, two meters, until he crashes and rolls on the ground.

Both men are out cold now. I turn to Zahira. She looks at me with shoulders bunched to her ears, mouth hanging open.

Then she turns and books it.

"Wait!" I try to follow her, but the world shrinks and squeezes my brain and I have to put a hand on the wall to stay standing. Pain rips up my side, like a running cramp but a thousand times worse. I shake my head, blinking and blinking again to push the dizziness away.

In the annoyingly long time it takes for me to recover, Zahira could have gotten away already. But luckily for me, there's a chain link fence on the other end of the alley, and Zahira is having a hard time even beginning to climb it.

"Wait," I say again, and manage a few steps towards her. "I'm not—I just saved you!"

She whirls around, pressing her back to the fence. Her eyes are filled with tears, which is just ridiculous. She definitely wasn't crying when the men were threatening her, but she's scared of *me?*

"Please," she says in a trembling voice. "I didn't see

anything. I swear."

"Wait. Just listen." I crouch down, careful not to pass out, and dig through Man #1's pockets until I find a simple black wallet. "I can pay you." I stand back up, this time really in danger of fainting. I squeeze my eyes shut and wish I could shout at the world to stop spinning. "I can pay you. I just need you to drive me to Ornament County."

Zahira stares at me, watery eyes flickering between my face and the wallet.

"I won't use my powers on you. Promise." I lift my hands like I'm surrendering. It seems like the right thing to do. "I just need a ride."

Zahira covers her eyes and crouches down, shaking her head as if trying to break out of a bad dream. "Oh my god," she breathes. "Oh my god." She looks up. At me. At the men on the ground. At the wallet. At me again. And buries her face in her hands.

She just might stay like that forever.

After a billion years, she gets up and stuffs everything back into her purse. She searches Man #2's pockets and fishes the cash out of his wallet.

"For the record," she says, pointing at me with the folded wad of money, "this is insane." She wipes her eyes. "Come on. Let's go."

She leads the way to her car as the men groan and start to wake. When we pass the diner, I say, "Hold on."

I hurry inside and see it there, on the pick-up counter: Zahira's hashbrown. I grab it, and the cashier yells, "Hey!" but I'm already out the door.

Zahira is standing beside her pink car, anxiously

tapping her foot and looking at the alley. When she sees me coming, she gets into the car and buckles up. I plunk into the passenger seat and try to catch my breath.

Zahira eyes my hashbrown.

"Do you still want this?" I ask.

She shakes her head, a little bewildered.

I nod. "Good."

And I devour it in three bites.

Well. I guess it was bound to happen.

Dear diary. The last page I wrote didn't end properly. It's because I saw two cops. I didn't really care at first, until I saw the papers they were showing around.

from a security camera   from photo day

Luckily Marisa was still in the washroom,

and I had my hat on. I was RIGHT THERE, and they didn't notice me at all.

The cops were asking around if people had seen us. They asked the ticket booth person. He said Marisa was "kind of scary" and "had a long coat" and "had a kid with her." That was enough for the cops. One of them said "They're around here somewhere. Set up a perimeter" into his walkie-talkie.

When Marisa came out of the washroom, I dragged her behind a vending machine so the cops wouldn't see her. I told her what I saw. I didn't know what to do, but Marisa had a plan, like she always does.

We had to move fast. The place was still crowded, but pretty soon people would start leaving, and we would be easy pickings. Marisa made me give her my hat and then picked a random guy in the crowd who had two kids with him and we stuck close to them, pretending we were one big family. She told me not to act so scared, but it was hard. It's like telling me not to shiver when it's cold.

But we made it into the parking lot. There

was a swarm of cops where we parked our car. We had to ditch it.

And then came the worst part. We managed to get out of the parking lot before the cops finished setting up their perimeter. We walked all the way into the city, staying with the crowd that was heading for the train. Marisa saw a mall and we went into the parking garage. She told me to spark one of the car's doors. I did. But then I saw what was in the back seat. One of those baby chairs. There were dolls and toys on the back and on the dashboard. We were stealing from a family with a baby.

I told Marisa we had to pick a different car, but she just told me to get in the car. I felt like crying. It seems stupid. But all I could think about was that family coming back from their shopping trip and realizing their car is gone. How are they going to get home? What if the baby is really really hungry or cold or sick?

What's more important: our lives, or some family we've never even met?

I don't know.

~~And I hate that I don't know.~~

ZAHIRA DRIVES FOR one solid hour before she finally speaks up.

"Just so we're clear," she says. Quiet, like her mind is floating somewhere far away, afraid of the answer. "You have...superpowers."

I watch her from the corner of my eye. I didn't really think about it before, but she has an accent. A foreign one, all fancy and cursive.

Outside the dry, warm bubble of Zahira's car, the rain has started up again, and the windshield wipers are like a metronome, telling me to *sleep, sleep, sleep*. I blink away my tiredness and sit straighter.

"Superpowers," I say. "Yeah."

"And you're...in some kind of trouble?"

"No."

"So you were at a truck stop all alone in the middle of the night because...?"

It doesn't matter, I want to snap. *You just have to drive.*

I guess she can tell I'm not interested in an

interrogation because she shuts up, leaving only the radio chittering away. It's tuned to the soft rock station. Good. The last thing I need is for her to hear a news report about The High School Incident and put two and two together and realize I'm the kid every cop in the province is looking for.

A few kilometers of rain splattering against the windshield and the wipers swishing their soggy lullaby later, she says, "If we pass a motel, I think we should stop for the night. I'm…" A pause as she holds back a bad word. Useless, because I don't care. "…tired. And I don't think I can keep driving for long like this. Not without driving us into a ditch."

She says it like a suggestion, but I can tell she wouldn't change her mind even if I had objections.

Before I can say *whatever*, she asks, "What's your name?"

The question comes so quick my mouth is still trying to form an answer to what she said before. What comes out is a stuttering, "Uh."

"And how old are you anyway?"

I scowl. She doesn't need to know any of this.

"Well?" she presses. Why is she brave enough to be grilling me all of a sudden? An hour ago she was crying because she was so scared of me. "You're, what, nine?"

"*Eleven.*"

"Oh, yeah?" She says it like she doesn't believe me, but it's true. I turned eleven yesterday.

"And my name is Dany," I add crossly.

"I'm Zahira."

"I know that."

"Well, good then." She does that thing again, where she looks like she wants to roll her eyes but doesn't. "And where did this..." *Superpower,* she means, but what she actually does is waggle her fingers. "Where did this come from? How did that happen?"

"It doesn't matter."

"Oh, it does." Her eyes are wide to drive home the point. "If I'm going to be taking you all the way to Ornament County, I deserve to know at least an iota of what I'm dealing with."

I scrape a sigh through my teeth and sink my head against the seat. She's not going to give up until she gets an answer. I just know it. If an answer could make her shut up until we reach a motel, then I would gladly throw her one.

But I don't know how I got the sparks. Marisa never had the chance to really explain it to me before she—well, she just never had the chance, and what she *did* tell me is mangled with the memory of us lying back-to-back, cold to our bones, her breathing all rocky and thick from being sick, and I don't want to think about that, so I try to focus on one thing. One name.

Suddence.

A little town in the middle of nowhere.

The town where Marisa grew up.

The town where I was born.

The town I'm trying to reach. The town I *need* to reach.

Where did my power come from? How did it happen? Maybe I'll find answers there. Maybe I won't. But I need to try to get there. It's the least I can do.

The wipers swish against the windshield and thud to a stop. Swish, thud. Swish, thud.

I have no answers to give Zahira. So I say the thing I hate the most.

"I don't know."

That can't possibly be enough for her, but she doesn't ask any more questions.

Swish, thud. Swish, thud.

I don't want to fall asleep next to a stranger. But the passing streetlights smear into the streaks of rain, and I close my eyes.

Dear Diary,

We've been driving for hours now. It's almost midnight. Marisa told me to go to sleep, but I'm afraid if I fall asleep, it'll make her fall asleep too. So I'm writing to keep myself awake. I don't know what to write about though. Just blah blah blah and bleh bleh bleh.

Here's a sad thing. We left our luggage and stuff in our car. But now it's confiscated by the cops, so it's all gone. All we have left is whatever is in my backpack and Marisa's bag. Luckily Marisa converted all our coins into dollar bills and she carries them around all the time. And I still have my special coins, which is good.

A list of everything we left behind:

- My pretty bomber jacket :(and all our clothes
- Marisa's phone charger
- My fancy pencil crayons I got for cheap at a thrift store
- Our rain boots (the forecast said it'll rain soon so that sucks)
- My binoculars
- My basketball
- Marisa's medicine

That's probably the worst part. Marisa doesn't know that I know she takes medicine, but I do. She hides in the bathroom when she thinks I'm still asleep in the morning and takes them. I don't know where she got them from. She has a bit of the medicine in her purse, but most of it is in our luggage. It sucks. I don't actually know what they're for, but they've got to be important. I hope we have enough money to buy more. We didn't get to go back to the casino to collect what we won :(We tried to. But when we drove past, the cops were already there.

I asked Marisa why we had to take this car. There were so many others in the parking lot.

She said it's because she JUST saw the family leave the car, so it would be a while before they came back, which would give us at least an hour before the car gets reported missing. That makes sense. But I'm still kind of mad. We stole from a baby, and she doesn't even seem sorry about it.

I guess she could tell I was still mad because she said she was sorry. She promised that once we ditch the car, the cops would return it to the family anyway, and the baby could have all the toys and dolls back, and the family would have all their stuff back. That did make me feel a little better. But I was still sad. I kept imagining the family coming back and seeing their car was gone. If that were me, I would just start crying. I don't understand why Marisa never cries. Or seems to be upset or scared or nervous. It must be a grownup thing.

She could tell I was still sad, so she gave me the Ultimate Offer. She would buy me french fries and ice cream to make it up to me. She asked "would that be okay" as if there would ever be a time when it isn't okay. And I'm not going to lie. It did make me feel a lot better.

MY MIND DRIFTS AWAKE when Marisa gently shakes my shoulder. I scowl and shrink farther into the warmth of my hoodie. "One more minute," I murmur.

A pause. A sigh.

"You'll sleep better inside. Come on."

Not Marisa.

Sleep drains away fast. Not Marisa. But she was here just now. She was right beside me, and we were talking...we were talking about something. Something important.

Wake up, Dany. Marisa's gone.

Marisa's gone.

Marisa's gone, and her absence cuts a black hole in my heart. I could bleed and bleed and bleed and it wouldn't bring her back but I wish it could because I miss her. I miss her so, so, so much.

I don't cry. I manage not to.

Not when I get out of the car.

Not when I follow Zahira to our motel room.

Not when I lock myself in the bathroom.

When I lean back on the door. When I sink to the ground. That's when the tears come, and I wish they could drown the whole world with me.

PART II:
Emergencies Only

Dear Diary,

Sad to report that I fell asleep anyway. Marisa drove through the whole night. She's sleeping now. But only because I practically begged her to. Otherwise she probably would have kept driving until she passed out and drove us off a cliff.

We stopped by this dusty little gas station to get supplies. We were both really thirsty. I told Marisa to nap in the car and I'll go buy some stuff from the convenience store. (She gave me $50.)

The store kind of sucked. It was super stuffy and there was no air conditioning. There was just one fan that I'm pretty sure is supposed to spin around, but it was stuck pointing at the cash counter. But the cash lady was nice. She was so big and muscular. She could probably lift a tree, like one of those lumberjacks. I should get muscles like that! She asked if I was alone, and I told her we were on a road trip and my "mom" drove through the whole night and she gave me money to buy things so she can nap a little. That's not really a lie. Marisa is basically my mom. She adopted me when I was a baby. The cash lady said "Aren't you a good kid" :) and then said I could "roam around."

≶THE HAUL≶

- Three packs of gum (sometimes we're non-stop travelling so much we don't have time to brush our teeth)
- Pocket tissue (some public bathrooms don't have toilet paper :/)
- Wet wipes and hand sanitizer (for when there aren't washrooms AT ALL)
- Phone charging cable
- Tiny tiny bottle of painkiller (kid-safe)
- A few bottles of water (VERY heavy)
- Bottle of coffee for Marisa (she likes caramel)
- Granola bars and energy bars
- And my ≶SECRET CANDY≶

Don't tell Marisa please. It was only $1.

There was a TV playing the news and it was showing those pictures of me and Marisa again. It was on mute so thankfully the cash lady couldn't hear it. The captions said the cops were "on the lookout" and that I was "abducted" and "do not approach." That last one is some good advice. Approach and get SPARKED. Approach and EAT BULLET.

The cash lady wasn't watching it, but just in case, I sparked the antenna juuuust a bit so it would only get static. She put everything in a paper bag for me. She also gave me a red candy! It was cherry flavoured.

When I went back to the car, Marisa wasn't napping AT ALL. She was talking on her cellphone. I tried to spy on her, but she saw me and hanged up. I was a bit mad at her because one of our cardinal rules is that our cellphones are for emergencies ONLY. Marisa shouldn't get to break the rules just because she's a grownup. We made the rules TOGETHER. I know who she's talking to. It's that woman from the clinic, Lilian. I don't even know why Marisa calls her. She's only met her like, once. Anyway, she was breaking another cardinal rule: never talk to anyone from the clinic.

At first I didn't ask about it because she was tired, and I bought secret candy so that makes us even. But this isn't the first time she called Lilian. And she always does it when she thinks I'm asleep, and she speaks very quietly, so I don't know what they even talk about. It isn't fair. If I tried to call Daniel or Lory or Curtis, Marisa would say I'm "not allowed." When I told Marisa we weren't supposed to call anyone, she said it's "just Lilian" like that makes it different. We could get CAUGHT, aka the THING WE'RE TRYING NOT TO BE. Marisa promised it's the last time she would call, and then she deleted Lilian's number. I told her that doesn't prove anything because she could have memorized it, and she said "You know I'm bad with numbers." I guess that's true. I never asked her for math homework help because she does math sooooo slow.

I checked her phone just to be sure. Usually she doesn't let me touch her phone, but she's sleeping, so it's not like she'll ever know. At least she's telling the truth. The contacts are completely empty.

Still though. She could have written down the number somewhere else. Or maybe Lilian's number is super easy to remember. Whatever. There isn't anything I can do about it. But next time she calls, I'm 500% spying on her.

because I never bothered to organize any of it. But what matters is the plastic candy tube at the bottom, still there, still intact. I don't take inventory of what's inside *that*. I can't bear it right now.

I fish the first aid kit from the side pocket and take a deep breath. Time for the ordeal.

I slowly take off my wet and grimy outer clothes. My red hoodie definitely needs washing. So do my jeans, really, but I know they'll take too long to dry. I toss them both to the ground for now, but I keep the key on a string around my neck. I don't want to put it down and have it fall down a drain pipe.

And then, carefully, I tug off my T-shirt and peek at the bandages around my waist.

Good thing: the bandages haven't soaked through. At least, I *think* that's a good thing. I snip the gauze away with the little scissor attachment on my army knife and force myself to actually look at the wound. It's not deep, but it looks bad. It *smells* bad. *That's* not a good sign.

I shouldn't, but I squeeze and pull at the swollen mess, just a little bit. Sure enough, there's still a sharp pain under the constant ache. I'm almost 100% sure there are splinters stuck inside. But the thought of digging into it with the army knife makes my knees turn to jelly, so I just soak the oozing wound with an iodine pad and cover it all up with fresh bandages.

It doesn't matter, anyway. I just have to make it to Suddence. Then everything will be okay.

Now that *that's* out of the way, I swallow one of my carefully-rationed painkiller pills and turn on the shower. The sputtering motel water has trouble getting hot, but once it does, letting it run over my hands almost makes me forget the pain.

Or maybe that's the medicine kicking in.

I'm too chicken to get water on my wound, so I just scrub my hair and wipe my body down with a wet towel and while I rinse out my hoodie, I try to figure out a way to break the news to Zahira.

I don't know where Suddence is.

I can imagine her response already. *You're telling me to drive you somewhere, and you don't even know where it is?* And her eyes would be all big and her thick eyebrows squashed down like she's one of those bad actors on TV.

But that's not totvolitially true. I *do* know where it is *approximately*. If I could get my hands on a map, I'm sure I can find it. How hard could it be? Ornament County can't be that big. I just have to look for a big blob of absolutely nothing, and smack in the middle of it, that's where Suddence will be. I think. I hope.

But I could be wrong. And I could look stupid. And I don't want to tell her that I don't know.

But I don't *need* to tell her I don't know.

I hold on hard to that. I don't *need* to tell her. Because I never wanted her to come with me, anyway. I only wanted her to get me close enough, and I'll figure out the rest from there. On my own, as it should be.

I squeeze out the water from my hoodie and hang it on the curtain rod to dry along with my rain-damp jeans and T-shirt. When I come out of the bathroom in my clean clothes, Zahira is sprawled on the bed, one arm over her eyes. I was hoping she might be asleep, but then she lifts her arm and squints at me.

"Finally," she grumbles, and sits up. On the bedside desk, she has already emptied the wallets we took from Man #1 and Man #2 and sorted the cash into bills and coins. "Oi. Before you go to sleep. Where in Ornament are we going?"

Uh oh. The dreaded question. Good thing I already figured this out in the bathroom. "You can drop me off anywhere," I say, hooking my backpack on the footboard.

She gives me a *look*. "Ornament's pretty big."

"I know." I didn't.

"And you want me to drop you off…anywhere."

I act confused about why she's confused. "…Yeah?"

"And then you're going to, what, walk?" She juts a finger at the front door. "With those shoes?"

I glance at my sorry excuse for sneakers. The wet duct tape is limp on the doormat like a dead animal.

I nod. "Yeah."

She huffs and says, "No way."

I scowl. *Why not?* is just on the tip of my tongue, but why would I ask? I don't need her permission. "I'll just fix them again," I say. "Duct tape's not that expensive."

"You think that's what I'm worried about?"

"I don't need you to *worry*."

It comes out so mean I instantly feel bad, even if Zahira doesn't look hurt by it, just surprised. I curl my fists and squeeze my eyes shut for a second. Be calm, Dany. If you make her mad, she might just run off with the money.

"You just need to drive me and drop me off," I say. Slowly, because I can feel the urge to snap bubbling up again. "That's all you have to do."

Zahira takes in a breath like she's about to say something, but then pauses for so long she might have given up on saying it.

I can't help my impatience. "What?"

Carefully, she says, "I didn't want to ask you before because it seemed personal, and you seemed upset." I still am, but clearly that's not stopping her. "But are you…alright? Are you safe?"

I don't say anything, which is apparently an answer all on its own.

"If you're in trouble," she says, "you need to tell me."

"Or what?"

Her eyebrows snap down, like she can't believe I have to ask. "Or I won't know how to properly help you."

"I'm not in trouble."

"So, all this." She circles her cheekbone. I know she's talking about the red scratches and already-fading bruise on my face. "You, what, fell down the stairs?"

I didn't. I didn't get hit, either, which I know is what she's thinking.

"It was an accident," I say, and goddamn hope this is the last thing she's going to grill me about. "Nobody did this to me."

She sighs. Not in a sad way, but in an angry way. No, not quite angry. Frustrated, like she doesn't believe me, but I don't know what I'm supposed to tell her. *Oh, I got caught in an explosion, no big deal.* Yeah. Like that'll make her shut up.

"Look," she says. "I'm asking because it's the middle of the night, and you were all alone in that diner. Is there nobody traveling with you? Where are your parents?"

"They're dead." I try to keep my mind on my real parents, the ones I never knew. "It was a long time ago."

Zahira looks sad and unsurprised. It makes my chest burn.

"Like I said. You don't have to worry about me." I push the blanket down the bed with too much force and climb in. I don't like the idea of sleeping beside a stranger, but one bed was all we could afford, and I'm absolutely not sleeping on the ground. "And I'm not alone. Someone's waiting for me in Ornament. Someone who can protect me. So you don't have to worry. I'm safe. I'll be safe." And even if I wasn't, what's she going to do? Run Them over with her janky pink truck? I don't think so.

Zahira stares at me like she can't decide if she wants to believe me. But it's not long before she lifts her shoulders and says, "Okay," and begins gathering up the cash on the desk. "I'll be level with you. I don't know how to get to Ornament. So first thing tomorrow, we're going to find a map, and we're going to figure this out. Got it?"

I roll my eyes but say, "Got it."

"This should be enough to get us there. For petrol and motels and food." She eyes the doormat. "And a pair of shoes."

"I said I'll fix them."

"And I said we're buying you a pair of shoes," she says, like that settles it.

"Fine." I roll over and pull the blanket up to my ears. "Your loss, anyway."

Dear Diary,

We're safe at a motel now. When we got here, Marisa told me to stay put, and then she went to buy hair dye. She said she wanted to get my ice cream french fries too, but the ice cream machine was broken. I told her it's okay. We better save our money right now. And it's not The Ultimate Treat without the ice cream anyway.

She bought some frozen hamburgers from the motel office instead. I wonder how long they've been frozen. I hate microwave food because they're always so soggy. But complaining makes me sound like such a baby, so I just ate it as fast as I could. There was mustard in it :(

The hair dye was blonde. I was hoping it would be a cooler colour. I keep telling Marisa she should dye her hair blue, or let ME dye my hair blue, but she always says no. It's sad. But I get it. We're supposed to be ~inconspicuous~. When this is over I'm so dyeing my hair blue.

Marisa got me to help dye the back of her head. She had to bleach it first. It smelled like burning. It was disgusting. And it was all slimey and hot.

The first time Marisa changed her hair, she didn't have to bleach it. She just dyed it a darker brown, almost black. It used to be caramel colour on the bottom half. To me she didn't look any different. But maybe it did work because we went a long time without any cops noticing us. This time she's going all blonde, and she said she would style her hair to be straighter, which sucks. I like how curly her hair is. My hair is curly too, but not like hers. More loopy and swoopy than curly.

I had to wear gloves when using the bleach.

They were weird and powdery. They made my hands really sweaty.

The original plan was to cut my hair, which is what we did the first time too, but I really REALLY wanted to try dyeing it. But I knew she would say no if I asked straight up, so I tried dropping hints and asking things like "why do I have to cut my hair" and "how come YOU don't have to cut your hair" and "you never ask me if I want to dye my hair."

Okay, that last one was a little obvious. But the important thing is that she got my hint and agreed to dye my hair!! There wasn't enough bleach to dye my whole head, so she gave me streaks. She said it's my early birthday present :)

But part of the deal is that I can only have it for a few days, when we're laying low in this motel. And then we're cutting my hair. That's fine. At least I'll be cool for a few days.

Hopefully this time she won't cut it too short. The first time, I was basically bald. I felt like an egg. But Marisa made it clear it was either I cut my hair so I don't get recognized, or They find me and vivisect me.

Vivi = Alive

Sect = Cut apart

Who the heck wants that!!!!

Sorry. I realized I never explained who They are. You must be so confused.

They (with a capital T) run the clinic that Marisa took me to after I pushed over Johnny McKay at school. Nobody believed that I didn't touch him, and nobody cared that he had it coming. He was bullying the new kid and stomping all his stuff into the mud. AND the week before he bit one of my tangrams but I was the one who got into trouble for shouting and "not using my inside voice." The principal wanted to suspend me, but Marisa came and withdrew me instead. SHE believed me. And the day after that, she took me to the clinic. At first I thought she didn't actually believe me and was getting me tested for anger problems, but she said she searched really hard to find a special doctor who deals with this kind of stuff. Doctor Heed was nice (WAS) and he really did believe me. When he asked me if I could do it again though, nothing happened. When I pushed Johnny McKay it was like my hands were on fire. They went numb, but there was that really painful pins and needles feeling like if you sat on your leg for too long and finally let it go and if you try to move it, it just feels unbearable and bad. The feeling went all the way up my arms and I wanted Johnny to feel that too. I wanted him to BURN. I made the pushing motion because I was so angry, and I imagined hurling the fire at him, but I didn't know it would ACTUALLY do something.

Anyway, this isn't about stupid Johnny McKay. The point is I couldn't make that burning feeling happen again, so Doctor Heed sent me back home with some "mind fullness" (??) exercises to try. It was just a bunch of breathing exercises and thought exercises to help me focus my mind. Marisa helped me with them. She also started homeschooling me, which was fine because I never want to see Johnny McKay again anyway. At first I thought maybe I could make the sparks come out by being angry again, but Marisa told me it was a bad way to do it because that makes it ~~"folitile" (Voletile?)~~ "volatile" (yes I had to ask Marisa how to spell that) and hard to control in the future. The whole point was to make it SO my sparks don't explode whenever I get mad.

Anyway, we did all those exercises about ~calming my mind~ and ~feeling every muscle in my body~ and eventually I could bring out my sparks whenever I wanted to. I could even spark things from three meters away (that was a big deal back then okay). Marisa took me back to the clinic, and we did a bunch of tests for like, a week, and Doctor Heed seemed very impressed. He asked if I would like to meet other kids like me. It would be like summer camp. We would hang out and get to know each other and have fun, and maybe my power would become even better. I said yes. I didn't even know there WERE other kids like me. That's when I met Lilian. Doctor Heed said she was one of the camp counsellors. She was nice too. She smiled a lot.

But then, while I was in the waiting room and Marisa was talking to Doctor Heed, she found out there was no camp. There was no "getting to know the other kids like me." They were going to keep me locked up and experiment on me. They were going to cut me apart and find out how my power works and then use it to do bad things. Marisa came out of Doctor Heed's office and told me to get my stuff from the car. But when we were at our car, she told me to buckle in, and then she just drove away. She was all nervous and I remember I thought I did something wrong. I kept asking what happened. She didn't tell me until we were at a motel a few hours away. It was probably the scariest thing I've ever heard. I can't believe I believed Them. They almost got me.

That's when Marisa chopped all my hair off and dyed her hair dark brown.

I can hear Marisa blowdrying her hair, so it's almost my turn to shower. She wrapped my streaks in tin foil so I wouldn't touch them, but I peeked in the mirror. It's hard to see through all the white goop, but I definitely see some orange in there!

I'll end it here. I'll let you know how my

hair looks tomorrow :)

    JUST KIDDING I'm back to report that my
hair looks ⸠AMAZING⸡

I'M SUDDENLY WIDE AWAKE. It's only seven in the morning. Zahira is still sleeping away.

Outside, the rain is heavy. It sounds like tiny stones pelting on the crappy motel roof. I curl up and try to go back to sleep. I try to think about the road, the cars whooshing by, the radio music. I try to think about Suddence.

Yesterday, trudging on the side of the highway, low-burning pain radiating from my side, the rain and cold soaking me all the way down to my bones, Suddence seemed impossible to reach. But now I have a way to get there, and it almost doesn't seem real. I could be there by tonight. Or tomorrow. Or the day after.

Soon.

Soon, and the idea should have been comforting.

But the rain is too loud, and my heartbeat is too fast, and I feel sick and my stomach hurts.

I find my way to the bathroom in the bluish seven A.M. dark. I don't even bother turning on the lights. I just find the toilet and...well. It sucks. But at least my stomach doesn't hurt anymore.

I scrub my hands with soap and wash my face with the cold, cold water. I flip on the lights. In the mirror, I look thinner. And paler. And my hair is too long. Marisa didn't get the chance to cut it. The streaks are still there, a dull orangey-gold, and I untangle them from my brown hair to see them better.

Last week, I stood in front of a motel mirror just like this, excitedly pointing to where I wanted the streaks to be, and Marisa pretended she wasn't happy about it, but I knew she was only teasing me because I caught her smiling in the reflection.

Last week.

How was it only last week? How was I so different? How was I so happy?

Before I can change my mind, I find my army knife and saw the streaks off.

I don't feel better. I didn't realize I was expecting to until now, gripping the dismembered hair, my nails digging into my palm. Something curdles in my chest, and I just stand there, trying to remember my breathing exercises, until I realize it's anger. Deep, deep, deep anger. And disgust. And horror. Because I wanted to feel better, and my first thought was to cut Marisa away. To try to *forget* her. How could I ever think that? How could I be so—

So—

My arms are burning up to my collarbones, and my ears are buzzing and ringing, and I know something bad will happen if I don't get a grip of myself. Breathe, Dany. Inhale—

One. Two. Three. Four. Five.
Exhale—
One. Two. Three. Four. Five.
Inhale…
Exhale…
When I don't feel so hot and shaky and the sparks
don't feel one wrong breath away from splitting free, I cut
the rest of my hair off.

Dear Diary,

We're officially in the ⌐fun⌐ part of being on the run: laying low.

"Wow, that sounds fun!" NO. It's fun for like, the first day. No waking up early? No constant driving? No peeing in gross gas station washrooms? Sounds amazing! But don't be tricked. It's only fun when there's good stuff to watch on TV.

Marisa says we only have enough money to be here for a few days. And then: I don't know. All of our plans are scrambled. We have to figure out a way to make back our money. But it's hard to do that when all the cops are on high alert.

We just had motel muffins for breakfast. Our lunch is probably more frozen burgers. I think it's weird when on TV, they show kids not liking vegetables. I would kill for a broccoli right now. I would even eat it RAW.

Basketball doesn't start until 4 o'clock, so I don't know what to watch. I keep switching through the channels and hoping they'll play something cool. But it's like they know I'm watching because everything they're playing is sooooo boooringggggg.

Marisa's hair still gets curly...
no idea what she's reading...
sss
This is noodle
I love you....
A B C
abcdefghijklmmopqrstuvwxyz
M
M
No I love YOU
raisin
APPLE
you will NOT believe what this says
STILL reading...
MOBY

The cooking show is kind of fun, actually. I like watching all the chefs get yelled at, even though 99% of the time I don't really get what they did wrong. Except the creme brulee one. I know how to make THAT. Marisa and I made it once. She even let me use the blow torch :)

Agh, but I haaate waiting a week for the next episode. AND there's no guarantee that we'll have a TV this time next week. We'd probably be driving, or maybe we'd get one of those cheap motels that doesn't have a TV. Or worse, we could be living in the car again. I hate laying low but now I'm secretly hoping we'll still be laying low next week so I can see the next episode.

Tuesday 11am channel 52

Now there's really nothing to watch except this show about high school and singing. Some of these people definitely don't look like highschoolers.

I've never been to high school. I mean, I

think that's pretty obvious. I'm ten years old (BUT I'M TURNING ELEVEN IN A FEW DAYS). Sometimes I don't know if I should be happy or sad about that. The homework seems so much harder. Everybody on TV talks about trigonometry (I had to ask Marisa how to spell that too) and algebra and calculus. I don't even know what those are. I hope it's like geometry. I like geometry.

But the cafeteria looks like fun. It's like an all-you-can-eat buffet. I don't think there are actual food fights though. We love food too much in real life to be chucking it like that. And the science class looks so fun and wacky. I know it's probably not like that in real life too, but it HAS to be more fun than what I did in elementary school. All we did was make oobleck and mix sugar water and salt water and whatever. Once the teacher made us bite plasticine. DISGUSTING. One time she got all dressed up like a real scientist in a lab coat and everything and made something called "elephant toothpaste" in a giant beaker. THAT was the only cool experiment, and WE didn't even get to do it. We were only allowed to watch. I hope in high school they give me the COOL stuff, like acid. Apparently dissecting frogs is a thing. Sounds interesting, but I'm not so sure if I want to do that.

I thought about asking Marisa if she ever did that, but she doesn't like to talk about herself, especially stuff from when she's younger. I think she doesn't like thinking about her parents :(I can't really imagine her as a highschooler. She's so serious. I know she's not ACTUALLY serious all the time. I can tell when she's feeling lighter and when she's feeling heavier. But I feel like a highschooler is supposed to have emotions on their face. On TV they're always crying or being angry and rebellious. Was Marisa ever rebellious? I can't imagine that either. But I also can't imagine her being bossed around by her teachers and parents.

There was another movie I saw that was about high school and singing AND basketball. That one was a lot of fun. Every time I switch through the channels I hope they're playing it, but I'm not so lucky today. I wonder if I could sing and play basketball. I think it would be pretty hard. Maybe their lungs are just super strong. Anyway, I don't think high school basketball is really like that in real life. But I WISH it was.

There's a basketball court at this motel. Usually Marisa would let me play if nobody else was outside. But now we're ~laying low~ so I'm not allowed to go outside AT ALL. I hate it. It's so nice and sunny. It rained a little last night so the court is kind of wet, but I don't really mind that.

Two kids just started playing there. I'm

not even allowed to watch them play because Marisa is afraid someone will look through the window and see me. But I can hear them playing. I can hear the ball bouncing and hitting the backboard.

~~Dear diary, I don't know if I can do this anymore. It was so CLOSE to being over. If we just had time to get what we won at the game. We could be out of the country by now. We could be finding a house to live in and looking at schools. We were so close. It makes everything feel so much worse. We've only been in this motel for a day and I already can't stand it. We don't have our stuff. We don't have our money. We're back at the start. Is it going to take another two years before we find another chance to make enough money? I don't want to do this. I don't want two more years of this. I just want it to be over.~~

"YOU CUT YOUR HAIR."

We're halfway across the parking lot, and it's apparently the first time Zahira noticed. But I guess I can't blame her. She *did* spend all morning squinting and moping like being awake is the hardest thing in the world, and I *did* shove my cap over my hair the moment I was done with it.

She unlocks her car and says, "Why?"

"I just wanted to." I crawl onto my seat with a shudder. It isn't raining anymore, but the air still feels wet. And cold. It's a cold that feels like it's drilling into every pore in my skin. And my hoodie still isn't dry. I guess that has something to do with it.

Zahira eyes me as she pulls on her seatbelt. "Don't you have a jacket?"

"I lost it." That's not true. Shoving it in the trash was very purposeful. I couldn't keep wearing it. People might have questions about the hole and the burns and the…everything.

"Are you cold?"

I'm very obviously shivering, but I say, "I'm fine."

Zahira squints in a way that says *I don't believe you* as she starts up the engine. The soft rock station blares on. In the engine's rumble, there's a weird gurgling. I can't remember if it was there last night. It might have been. I was too busy failing to stay awake to notice. I didn't realize just how old the car was last night, either, but that one's not on me. It was all dark and rainy and I couldn't see very well. But now that it's daytime, I can the rust on the edges of the engine hood, and the grimy cloudiness of the side mirrors, and the soggy leaves stuck at the bottom of the windshield, and the bald spots in the pink paint. When we clip the curb on the way out of the parking lot, the gurgling gets conspicuously worse.

"Is that normal?" I say.

"Is *what* normal?"

There's no way she doesn't hear it. But when I give her a pointed look, she just cuts me a scowl.

I say, "I think your car is dying, dude."

"Put on your seatbelt."

I do her the courtesy of shutting up and sitting back. We leave the suburbs and pass a long strip mall, and then we're out on the highway. It's all farmlands at first, all empty and grey and muddy, but then it turns into some kind of industrial district, and we're joined by a posse of trucks. I stare out the windshield, watching trucks go the opposite way on the other side of the highway, and start counting them.

One.

Three.

Seven.

Barely a minute later, I've already hit double digits, and the game is getting boring. I try to guess what each truck is carrying instead. It's a game that I used to play with—well, it's a game I used to play all the time. Sometimes it's obvious: wood planks, metal bars, logs. One carries a backhoe that looks dangerously close to falling off. Other times I have to look at the pictures on the side, or really pay attention to the company name. Emmy's Farm with its big red juicy tomato logo is probably carrying fresh fruits and vegetables. Warren's Moving Company is obviously furniture and boxes. It's the plain white ones with their LTD's and INC's and CO's that are hard to guess. All I picture are grey cement blocks.

On the other side of the highway, one of those long tow trucks whizzes by, and its double decker flatbed is filled to the tail with pickup trucks. *Filled.* I go back to my truck-counting game just to have the satisfaction of having the number jump up by ten.

The industrial area turns into more farmland, and the farmland turns into a farmer's market, and then we're in the next town. The truck population gets low. I spot two red ones and one black one before Zahira slows to perform the worst parallel parking I've ever seen.

"Got it," she says with satisfaction, turning off the engine, and I get the feeling this is one of her *better* attempts, and that honestly makes me a little concerned. "Get off. Let's be quick."

I slam the door shut and join her on the curb. I haven't really been paying attention to where we are, and I was expecting some kind of convenience store or gas station where we can buy a map, but when I look up at the store, I scowl.

"You're going to buy a map from a thrift store?"

Zahira is already halfway through the door. I hurry after her.

"I *said*," I hiss, quieter because there are other customers here, "you're going to buy a map from the thrift store?"

"No," she says lightly, picking through the racks of trousers. "We're buying you a jacket."

It takes everything not to stamp my feet like a baby. "I don't need a jacket."

"And I suppose you were just shivering from excitement in the car?" I open my mouth, but she doesn't give me the chance to answer. "You need a jacket, and you need a new pair of shoes. Go find something so we can get out of here and have some brunch."

I don't know what brunch is. But I know the only way to get Zahira off my case is to just pick a jacket and a pair of shoes, so I spin around angrily and trudge to the children's section.

But if I have to be honest, I do need a jacket. And I really do need a new pair of shoes. My left one is officially dead. The duct tape got lost somewhere in the motel parking lot, and now the sole flaps open every time I lift my foot.

I just hate that Zahira is right.

The size-five options all suck though, so I round the aisle to the size sixes and pick out a pair of white sneakers. I shove my hand inside one of them. Good. Arch support. Then I can walk longer without my feet hurting.

"Nice shoes." Zahira is peeking around the aisle, a basket in hand and a corduroy jacket slung over her shoulder. It's bright green.

"They're three dollars," I say, and scrunch my nose at the jacket. "I hope that's not for me."

"This?" She gives it a little jiggle. "Don't worry. It's for me."

"Good," I say, and head to the outerwear section.

Browsing through the jackets is harder than the shoes. They'll all jammed together onto a single rod, and if I pull one out to look at it, it's impossible to shove back in. It's a hell of a workout. Five jackets in, and my arms are already complaining. So instead of looking, I close my eyes and walk my fingers along the hangers until fate tells me to stop.

But the thing about fate is that it has no taste. Otherwise, it wouldn't have made me stop on the ugliest leopard-print jacket I've ever seen.

I try again and land on a red and blue puffy jacket. I'm about to unhook it from the rack when, a few hangers away, I see a trench coat.

I haven't cried since the bathroom incident. The trick is to never think about Marisa. Look out the car window. Pick a thing. Count. Think. Fill my brain with anything, as long as it isn't her. I thought I was doing pretty well.

But here, seeing this random trench coat in a random thrift store, it feels like a punch straight to my guts. Marisa always wore a brown coat like that. To pick me up at school. To go shopping. Every day of our run until we almost got caught at the stadium. Then she got rid of it, stashing it in the first trash bin we saw. *Too recognizable,* she said. *I should have gotten rid of it a long time ago.*

I tried arguing with her that she could still keep it. She just doesn't have to *wear* it. But she said it wasn't worth lugging around in our backpacks. It's just a coat.

When we drove away from the trash bin, I tried to remember how many turns and stops we made, the street names, any recognizable buildings, just in case I ever had the chance to go back and get it.

I never got the chance to go back.

And I can't even remember where it is.

"Dany?"

I don't know when Zahira appeared beside me. I look away so she won't see the tears welling in my eyes.

"Dany," she says again, slowly. "Are you okay?"

I nod, which is a bad idea because it nearly makes my tears fall.

She sighs through her nose and takes a long time considering what to say. "Well. I found this over there." She drapes a maroon hoodie on the rack. "It kind of looks like yours. I thought you'd like to have it."

I blink until my eyes are dry enough and glance at the hoodie. It does look like mine.

"And you chose this jacket, right?" She pulls it out of the rack for me and pats the wrinkles out of it. "Looks nice. Very fashionable. Only five dollars. Sure you want this one?"

I don't want to wipe my nose because it would give away that I'm crying, but at some point it's just impossible to sniff it all back up, so I rub my sleeve under my nose and pretend it's just itchy. I don't trust myself to say anything without bursting into tears, so I just nod.

Zahira takes me to the pants section, where she helps me pick out some grey jeans because she noticed mine are still damp with rainwater, and then I follow her to the counter and watch her slide our stuff to the cashier. My coat. My sneakers. My pants. Her disturbingly green jacket. And a strange little ceramic dog. It's not even one those novelty saltshakers you find in gift shops. It's just a straight up haunted statue that does nothing but stare into your soul with its scratched-up little eyes.

Everything rings up to seventeen dollars. Zahira tries to pay with her card, but it gets declined. As she grumbles and digs for her cash, I watch the cashier wrap the cursed dog in newspaper. Very, very slowly, like she has all the time in the world, which I guess she does because there's no one else in line.

And horribly, the newspaper she's using is the giant frontpage headline about The Motel Incident.

Even worse, under that giant frontpage headline is a giant picture of the messed-up motel parking lot, and in the corner of *that* are giant photos of Marisa and me.

I glance at the cashier. She's too busy searching for some tape.

I glance at Zahira. She's too busy counting out coins from her wallet.

When the cashier finishes the wrap job and places everything in a crumply gift bag, I take it before either of them can get a good look at the paper. Zahira pays, and on the way back to the car, I turn the wrapped statue around so the picture of me is face-down.

Dear Diary,

This morning I heard Marisa on the phone. She was in the bathroom. I KNEW she was lying about never calling Lilian again.

I know I promised I would spy on her. I tried. I basically had my whole ear on the bathroom door. But I still couldn't really hear what she was saying. She was speaking so quietly. I heard something like "I'm not going to meet you" and "Don't trick me." There was no way I could hear what Lilian was saying. All I really know is that she was making Marisa really mad.

I heard her hang up so I went back to bed and pretended to be asleep, but she was in there for a really long time before she finally came out. She told me she was going out to run "an errand" and that I could keep sleeping and I could have muffins for breakfast. I guess she decided to meet Lilian anyway. I almost asked why. But that would have been a bad move because then she would know I was spying on her and she would get mad.

But I should be the one getting mad! First she broke our rules and talked to Lilian. Then she lied about never calling her again. And now she's going to break our rules even MORE because she's GOING TO SEE LILIAN. As in LILIAN WHO WORKS FOR THEM.

I thought about following her, but she took the car. There was no way I could sneak into the back trunk without her noticing. So now I'm just here, being so mad at Marisa and watching stupid TV and eating a muffin. I'm not supposed to eat in bed because crumbs or whatever but WHO CARES. Marisa isn't even here.

Why does she even talk to Lilian? Did she

secretly know her before the clinic? Is that how she even found Doctor Heed in the first place? She found him pretty fast after my school incident. I should have known it was suspicious.

Sorry. I knocked you off the table. It was a hard fall. Some of your pages are bent now :(It was an accident, I swear. I was practicing my sparks. I'm supposed to practice only when Marisa is here so she can walk me through all the mind-fullness stuff and supervise me or whatever, but I don't care. She's not here. How is she ever going to know. And when I practice with her, she only lets me use small sparks. "Don't want to cause an accident blah blah blah" well, I just created a humongous spark. It's the size of my hand. And guess what? I called it up at least ten times, and not a SINGLE time caused an accident. (Except knocking you off the table. But that's a small accident. Marisa makes it sound like I'll blow up the whole place.) I would never get this far if I don't practice secretly. And what's the point of keeping it small, anyway? What if we get in trouble?

You know what's really really weird? I hate the clinic, but at least when I did those tests with Doctor Heed, I felt strong. I felt POWERFUL. I smashed through all these different woods and tiles and metals. I splintered a bulletproof glass! Yeah, my head hurt like hell afterwards and I fainted or whatever, but I bet I could have sparked through the glass. I bet if I practiced like that every day, we wouldn't even need to be afraid of cops, or even Them, because I could just blow them up in a millisecond. I wouldn't even get dizzy. I would be a goddamn superhero. I'm sure Marisa would LOVE my giant sparks then.

Great. Now my head hurts. I'm bored. I want to go outside. And I'm HUNGRY.

I just remembered the secret candy I bought (hehe).

I'm sorry to report that it tastes REAL bad. It's grape flavoured. It's like cough syrup. I'm so mad. I should have picked the other flavour. That one was green so it was probably green apple, which is my favourite flavour. I just wanted to try something new :(At least it was only a dollar.

Well. There's nothing else I can eat. Marisa said she'll be back at 12 with hot lunch. But that's a WHOLE NOTHER HOUR and I'm hungry NOW. We don't even have anything good to drink. We just have apple juice boxes (I already had one for breakfast) and whatever's in the kettle, but the water in there tastes like plastic. I think I would die if I keep drinking it. I guess I could drink the sink water. BUT DO I TRUST THE MOTEL PIPES??

I do have another option. It's a forbidden option. There's a vending machine outside (two, actually, one has snacks and one has liquids). I'm not supposed to leave the room. But Marisa isn't supposed to be meeting our enemy either. And guess what?!? She isn't here. And you won't tell, right? It's not like she ever reads you anyway. She never has to know.

Onto my snack quest! I'll be right back.

I PEEK INTO the first washroom stall. The toilet is clogged with a nest of toilet paper. In the second stall, the ground is covered in a slime of toilet paper soaked in mystery liquid. Well. I guess it's not that much of a mystery.

I go back to the first stall and flip the toilet lid down with the tip of my toe so I don't have to look at it. But when I close the door and go to hang my backpack, I realize a second horrible thing. This stall doesn't have a coat hook.

This has got to be the worst convenience store washroom I've been to. No, second worst. At least this one has locks that work.

"Zahira?" I say.

"What?" she says from the other side. Last I checked, she was touching up her eyebrows in the mirror.

I open the door. "Can you hold my backpack."

She makes a short humming sound and reaches for it without turning away from the mirror, taking a few tries before successfully grabbing my backpack. I take out my new clothes and duck back into the stall. The top of the toilet paper dispenser looks clean enough. Still, I wipe it off before putting my stuff there.

It's only when I take off my damp and starting-to-smell hoodie that I realize just how much my T-shirt reeks too. Of rainwater and sweat and greasy food.

I sniff my new hoodie. It smells like the thrift store, old and sweet. It smells *clean*. Suddenly I can't bear the idea of putting it over my disgusting shirt.

"Zahira?"

"What?"

"There's a shirt in my bag. Can you pass it to me?"

I hear her unzip my backpack and rustle through it. And then she pauses. "This ratty one?"

I wouldn't call it that, but I say, "Yeah."

"It's falling apart."

I scowl. It's not like she hasn't seen it before. I literally wore it last night. It's been my sleeping shirt for two years. "It doesn't matter. Just give it to me."

"You don't have any other tees?"

"No."

She sighs, and I can practically hear her half-eyeroll. "Hang on."

I hear her heading to the door, and I scowl again. "Where are you going?"

"Getting you a better shirt," she calls, and then the door clamps shut.

I have to bite back from yelling *I don't need a better shirt*. It would be annoying. And it would be a lie. I *could* use a better shirt. I hate admitting that.

Oh. And also, yelling would draw attention. Cardinal rule number four. Keep a low profile.

A few minutes later, Zahira comes back and waves a bunched-up shirt over the top of the door. "Shirt," she says.

I take it. It's an aqua tie-dye shirt with some kind of comic I don't understand printed on the front. It's ugly, so thank god it'll be hidden under my hoodie.

"You can keep it," she says. "I never wear that one."

Yeah, I can tell from the heavy smell of closet coming from the shirt. It's too big, but at least it's not thin and unravelling and filled with little holes.

I take off my gross shirt and tug on Zahira's. "Why do you just have a random shirt?"

"All my stuff is in my truck," she says. And after a heavy sigh, "I got kicked out of my apartment."

I remember hearing that. I don't want her to get mad at me for eavesdropping though, so I keep my mouth shut.

I pull on my new hoodie, and then my new jacket, and then my grey jeans. I already have my new shoes on. It's strange to feel so nice and warm after being cold and wet and miserable for so long. In a few days it won't matter. But for now, I'll take it.

I step out of the stall, and Zahira brightens. "Look at you! Those fit you well."

"Thanks." I give my new look a onceover in the mirror. Good. I don't look suspicious. I take my backpack from Zahira and start for the door.

Her phone rings. No, just a chime. A text message. I can tell it's from Aaron because Zahira takes one look at the screen and makes a face of absolute stink.

I stop at the door and watch her debate whether to reply or not. Another chime, and the stink turns into anger. She begins typing out a reply.

And keeps typing.

And keeps typing.

It's like she doesn't remember I'm standing right at the door, waiting for her to finish so we can leave this rancid little washroom. I try clearing my throat. I try opening and closing the door. Nothing.

"Zahira," I say.

"Hm?"

She didn't even look up. I cross my arms and give her the *look*. "Do you maybe want to save the lover's spat for later? We're kind of on a time crunch here."

"Just..." She flips a hand, still typing away. "Go pick out what you want for lunch. I'll find you later."

I guess I haven't really mastered the *look* yet. Clearly I'm not going to get her to unstick her eyes from her phone, so I kick the door open and trudge to the food section. Lunch? We haven't even had breakfast yet.

I pick out my usual convenience store meal, which is a cold wrap and a bottle of generic orange juice. I stop in front of the iced coffee before remembering— remembering that I don't know what coffee Zahira likes, or if she even likes coffee at all.

Speaking of Zahira, she still hasn't come out of the washroom. What can she possibly be texting Aaron? I thought they broke up.

I snag a basket from beside the entrance and run my mental road trip checklist. Giant bottles of water. A few energy bars. Tissue paper and wet wipes and hand sanitizer. I don't know if I need this much stuff. I don't know how long it'll take to get to Suddence.

I find a heavy book of maps on the bottom shelf and flip through it, trying to find where we are. But then I hear the washroom door open, and Zahira finally comes out.

She takes one look in my basket and says, "Why do we need all that?"

I can tell from her crankiness that she didn't make up with Aaron. Shocker.

I say, "How long does it take to get to Ornament?"

"Depends on traffic." She sticks her hands in her pockets. "I'd say two days. Three days, tops."

I think for a second and put back some of the energy bars and one big bottle of water. "That should be enough."

"Sure," she says. Flippantly, like she's taking my word only because she doesn't care.

Her phone rings. It's a proper ring this time. She doesn't even look at the screen. She just jams the decline button.

"Come on," she grouses. I read that word in a book once. It's not a word I think about a lot because it's weird, and I'm pretty sure it's also a bird. But there's no other way to describe how Zahira sounds right now. "Let's pay."

I lug the basket to the register. Zahira snatches a bottle of soda and asks the cashier for one of the oily rolling hotdogs at the counter. I wrinkle my nose at her lunch. I thought grownups are supposed to be obsessed with healthy food.

"And also, forty dollars of gas for pump number..." She squints out the window. "...two, please."

She pays, and we carry our stuff to her car in paper bags. Her phone rings again. This time she just lets it ring and ring until it stops.

I want to ask why she doesn't just block his number, but she has the absolute air of *don't talk to me,* so I bite the inside of my lips instead.

After we stuff the groceries into the car, Zahira goes to the gas pump, and I hang my feet out of the open passenger door and drum my heels on the bottom ledge of the car. The sun is peeking between the clouds, making the wet asphalt glitter. There's no warmth in it, though, and my sigh comes out in a cloud of white.

Zahira's phone rings again. This time she digs it out with a growl and flicks it open like a knife.

"You got something to say?" she snaps into it. "I'm all ears. Let's hear it."

Aaron's tinny voice says, "I just wanted to make sure you're okay."

"Yeah? And why *wouldn't* I be okay?" She stabs the pump into her car. I get the feeling she wishes she were stabbing something else.

"Look, I didn't want this to happen," Aaron says, and Zahira actually rolls her eyes this time. Not that half-roll I've seen her do. Her eyes go full white. "Those guys—I was just scared—"

"And you think *I* wasn't scared?" Zahira exclaims.

"I didn't—"

Zahira hangs up. And going by the extra buttons she's pressing, she just blocked Aaron.

I climb to the driver's side and roll down the window. "He sounds like a douchebag."

She frowns at me. "Where'd you learn that word?"

From Marisa. But I say, "TV."

"Don't you know it's a bad word?"

"What's the deal with Aaron?"

She hawks a laugh and noticeably doesn't answer.

"What did he do?" I lean farther out the window. A mistake, because it makes my side hurt, and it takes everything not to wince. I stick my hands in my pockets so I can press on my side without Zahira seeing. "Why were those two guys so mad at him?"

"Because..." She scrunches up her face. "You wouldn't get it."

"Why?"

"It's grownup stuff."

"I know grownup stuff."

Clearly that isn't good enough for her because she just keeps pumping gas.

But then she must have noticed me looking at her expectantly because she sighs and flips her eyes towards the sky.

"We met in school," she says, and knocks the pump against the gas valve to get every last drop. "He was nice. Funny. We were both in med, and we were both broke, so he said *we can figure it out together.*" She bobs her head as she impersonates him, doing a voice that sounds nothing like the one I heard over her phone. "Except he didn't do *anything,* and I was working all the time, and it still wasn't enough, so I finally decided to drop out, and *he*—" She makes an impatient sound, like she really, *really* needs to bite something. "He had the glowing idea of borrowing from some guys on the street. And obviously he couldn't pay them back, and—god, and he just *left.* If I ever see him again..."

She shoves the pump back into its socket. Her fist is clenched so tight around it her knuckles are shiny and white, and I get a picture of what she'll do if she sees him again. It's funny. She's wearing pink-rimmed sunglasses on top of her head, and they're heart-shaped, but she's so very much not in love right now.

She gets in the car and polishes off half her hotdog before I can even get the plastic wrap off my lunch. She shoves the rest between her teeth and unearths an old permanent marker from the glove box.

"Pass me that," she says through the hotdog, pointing at the book of maps. *Road Atlas,* it says.

I dig it out and pass it to her. She chows down on the rest of the hot dog until all that's left is a smudge of grease beside her mouth. Then she scrubs her lips with the back of her hand, and then *that's* gone, too.

She puts the atlas against the wheel and thumbs through it. "We are...here." She marks a spot and flips a few pages. "Ornament is here. I've driven to the border before. It took...yeah, it took two days. Less, probably. Where exactly are you going again?"

"Give me the book," I say, and take it from her. I scan the pages until I find it. Suddence. Smack in the middle of nowhere.

Zahira is busy taking big swigs of her soda. I point at the city nearest to Suddence and say, "Here."

She pulls the book back and squints at the town, her cheeks puffed with soda. We did an experiment in school once where we soaked chicken bone in soda for a week. It was supposed to show how the sugar and caffeine eats your teeth away. But what it really did was make me wonder if fizzy chicken soup existed. I thought about telling her gargling on soda like mouthwash will ruin her teeth, but I get the feeling she doesn't really care. About her teeth, and about what I say.

Finally she swallows the soda and says, "Okay. Ornament City. That's not that far from the border." She flips to a different page, a closer view of the town. "I can drop you off in the city center. Downtown. That alright?"

I nod, taking a small bite of my wrap.

Zahira draws a careful line through the book, following the roads and highways until the two locations are connected. She sits back with satisfaction. "There. We can cover most of it today, and the rest tomorrow morning. And we should have enough money for petrol and one night at a motel."

I take a small sip of my orange juice and wish I got something warm instead. "Why can't we drive through the night?"

She squints one eye. "Why would we?"

"No motel. Save money."

"I'm not dropping you off in the middle of the night." She actually sounds offended. "And news flash, I can't drive for twelve hours straight. I need to rest."

"Fine." I sit back and sip on my juice.

"And I need to keep driving east after I drop you off, so I *definitely* need to sleep."

That surprises me. Not the fact that she's driving east. The fact that I never thought about what she'll do after she drops me off. "Where are you going?"

"Home," she says. I get mixed feelings from the way she says it, like home is a good place, but she doesn't want to go there. "I was supposed to go back for the holidays, anyway."

A car honks as it pulls into the gas station, wanting Zahira's spot. Zahira does her half-eyeroll and tosses the atlas on my lap. "Keep me on track," she says, and starts the car with that terrible coughing gurgle. I give her a pointy look. Her response is flicking her heart-shaped sunglasses down from the top of her head.

I roll my eyes, which I'm sure doesn't look as impressive as hers, and kick off my new shoes so I can stretch out my toes. Once I navigate her to the highway, it's back to having nothing to do, so I flip ahead to our destination. There's only one road leading into Suddence, and it's a long one. How long would it take to walk there? A few hours? My side is already throbbing in protest at the idea.

Suddence. I don't know much about it, except that it's a small town. My mind goes immediately to those little seaside villages with colourful wooden houses sitting on short cliffs against the cold, grey sea. But of course, Suddence isn't by the sea. As far as I can tell, it isn't even near a lake. A little town in the middle of nowhere. What would it look like?

"Owhhh," Zahira suddenly says, her face all twisted up. At first I think she's in pain, but then she says, "I hate this song."

I haven't been paying attention to the music. I've heard this song a few times before. Not enough to totally know the lyrics, but enough to know it's a song about falling in love. Probably in a club.

"I like it," I say.

"*Really?*" She leans an elbow on the door and rubs her forehead. "It just makes me think of my stupid summer job last year. Actual flashbacks."

"Oh," I say.

"I used to work in a pizza shop in the mall," she says, even though I didn't ask. "Metro Place. You ever been there? It's like they only played the same five songs."

I go back to imagining Suddence.

"Oh my god," Zahira says out of nowhere. "Have you ever been to an arcade?"

I try to follow her path of thought but fail. "Huh?"

"The pizza shop. It was across from an arcade. I've been there a few times. I swear they rig all their machines. But have you, you know..."

She gives me a meaningful look through her pink-tinted sunglasses, and I get what she's talking about. "I've thought about it," I say. I really have. I've seen arcades on TV, and I fantasize a lot about how I would cheat the games with my sparks. It would be so easy. I would have enough tickets to trade for one of the big prizes. But I was never allowed to go, so I never got to try.

"There were these machines," Zahira says. "These moving platforms full of tokens. The whole conceit is that you have to put your token in at the right time, and it'll all get pushed off—hard to explain, but I bet you would do wonders at them. And the claw machines, you could just..." She flicks her fingers three times. "You wouldn't even have to put tokens in."

I press my lips against a smile. I've thought about that, too. "Yeah."

"Or even Skee-Ball, or...or those basketball games!

God, we could be a duo. We could make bank." She leans back in her seat contently. "Maybe before I drop you off, I can take you to that arcade, and we can try it out, yeah? It's only like, an hour away from Ornament City."

She's joking, but I can't help my smile now as I imagine the two of us running through the arcade, trailing long strands of tickets behind us. It's weird. I barely even know her. But maybe I *do* want to go with her. Maybe I *do* want to go to an arcade and cheat at every game.

But I can't. Even if it's only a few hours.

The thought stings. For a moment she almost convinced me it was a possibility. Like maybe we could just make a quick detour to her hometown before we part ways forever.

Too risky, says Marisa's voice in my head. Too risky, and she's right.

So before my imagination spirals out of control, I stamp it all out.

Dear diary.

I don't know how to start.

Something bad happened. It isn't my fault. But Marisa thinks it is. I can tell she's super mad at me because she won't talk to me.

But it ISN'T my fault. I didn't get caught because I went to look for the vending machine. Those cops were already there. The motel woman called them. They said so on the radio. I got a grapefruit energy drink thing and chips and I turned around and suddenly there was a cop there. He told me "it's okay" and was holding his hand at me like I'm some kind of rabid animal, and then he very obviously called for backup on his walkie-talkie, like I'd be too stupid to know what he was doing.

I tried to run. But one of his buddies showed up, and they tried to corner me. I didn't spark them. That's one of our cardinal rules: I should NEVER use my sparks on people, ESPECIALLY people who don't know I have superpowers. But I got lucky because there was a big gap between them and I just booked it. I went back to the motel room because I didn't know where else to go. I thought maybe Marisa would be back and she would save me. But she wasn't. I locked the door and called her on the motel phone. I told her what was happening, and she said she was coming back right away, and before she hanged up, I heard Lilian's voice. It was far from the phone and hard to hear, but it was definitely Lilian.

And then I heard the cops outside the door, and they were trying to break it down, and I panicked. It was like all of a sudden my mind went white and all I could think about was hiding. I grabbed my backpack. But I didn't take you. You were on the table and by the time I remembered you, I was already hiding in the bathroom, and the cops were kicking through the door. I know hiding in the bathroom was a bad move. I should have sparked through the windows and ran.

That's when it got worse. I was trapped in the bathroom and the cops knew it. They were knocking outside and telling me it's safe to come out, that they're there to help me, that they won't hurt me. I knew they wouldn't hurt me. But I wasn't afraid of them. I was afraid of Them. But how was I supposed to explain all that? They wouldn't believe me anyway. I told them to go away. I was so scared they were just going to kick down this door too, and they'll take me away from Marisa and then They'll find me.

Remember when I said my sparks are invisible? They're supposed to be. I can sort of see them, like if you stare at a light for too long and you see a purply shadow of it if you look somewhere else. That's what the sparks look like to me. But nobody else can see it. Doctor Heed recorded me during the tests. I looked at the video afterward. The sparks weren't there, even though I knew they were.

But in the bathroom, suddenly I could see them. I wasn't calling to them. They just appeared. They were so bright and flashing off my hands and the walls. I could feel something really bad was about to happen. I could feel the sparks about to explode.

But I controlled it. I tried to tell Marisa that. I don't think she believes me. I put up my hands and imagined all the sparks coming between them, and they did. But they still wanted to explode, so I told them to go. I pushed them at the door and blew it right up. I don't know what happened to the cops on the other side. I just ran.

But there were more cops in the parking lot. A whole bunch of them, with guns and squad cars. It's like they just appeared. The guy in charge told me not to be afraid and they have the place surrounded. You're not supposed to say that together. How is anyone supposed to be not afraid when you basically just told them they can't leave.

I could feel the sparks starting again. They weren't visible yet, but I could feel the pins and needles all the way up my arms, and my head was buzzing too. I knew I had to get out of there fast, before the sparks blew again and the cops saw what I can do. But there wasn't anywhere I could run. They had me trapped.

The guy in charge tried to talk to me. He told me to come with him and they could keep me safe. I'm not supposed to talk to cops, but I couldn't help it. I told them they don't even know what they're supposed to keep me safe from. They still think Marisa kidnapped me. They'll never believe what Doctor Heed and his goons want to do to me.

I wasn't planning to spark them, but then I heard one of their walkie-talkies. They were talking about Marisa. She was coming back to the motel, and they were going to get the jump on her.

I'm not supposed to show my sparks to anyone. But I wanted, WANTED them to burn.

I let the sparks fill me up with fire, and then I screamed. I didn't aim for the cops. I aimed for their cars. They got blasted way up in the air, and there were burn marks on the ground, and the cops got blown back. I've never seen my sparks like that before. Never that big, never that bright, and they were hot, like they were real explosions with real fire. Calling them made me dizzy and I tried to run, but one of the cops grabbed me. I tried to spark him off. I didn't care about our rules anymore. But it was like I used them all up. I didn't feel the pins and needles. I just felt all numb and sick.

And then Marisa came. She drove right over the curb to get into the parking lot and told me to get down. I did, and she shot the cop grabbing me. I don't know if she shot him dead. But I felt his blood on my neck.

Marisa got me onto the car and I passed out.

We're safe now. We've been driving for a while. But dear diary, I left you behind. I'm sorry. I should have remembered you. I should have grabbed you before I ran. But I'll keep writing you in my head, I promise. I'm sorry. I'm so, so sorry.

I DON'T REMEMBER falling asleep, but all of a sudden I'm snapping awake to something that sounds like it could be used as a pterodactyl screech in a movie. It's already getting dark, the bluish-grey evening punched through by streetlamps and headlights. I scowl out the window. Which idiot left their handbrake on?

A second later, I realize the sound is coming from *our* car.

"Oh my god," Zahira says, suddenly sitting straight. The car jerks back and forth, throwing me like one of those mechanical bulls I always see in carnival scenes on TV. I sit straighter too and try to see if the engine is on fire, but I don't see any smoke over the dashboard. I've never really thought about what a dying car might sound like. But this gurgling, sputtering, grinding cry seems about right. You're not supposed to stop on the highway, but Zahira pulls over. The little meters on the dashboard are going nuts, flashing a million different warnings that can't possibly all be happening at once. The car stops with a bump so forceful I thought we might flip over.

And then the engine dies.

The silence comes so quickly that my ears ring. No engine. No radio.

Slowly, the sound of the outside world leaks in. The drizzle on the windshield. The whoosh of cars passing by. The wind in the trees.

Then Zahira mutters, "Oh, shit," and shoves the door open.

I thought about following her. But it's so warm inside the car, and it's raining outside, and it's not like I know anything about fixing cars. I sink back in my seat and watch her shuffle to the front of the car with her pink jacket held over her head. She wrenches open the engine hood, which makes an awful creak, the perfect sound for a *baby* pterodactyl.

I can't see her anymore, so I wait to hear her start tinkering with the machinery. But I think she's just standing here because I don't hear anything happening.

I groan and slink out of the car. Zahira really is just standing there, one hand propping open the hood, one hand holding the jacket over her head. She has a pinched-eyebrows, bunched-lips concentrated look, but I can't help but notice she's not actually *doing* anything. She doesn't even have a flashlight.

I lean my arms on the edge of the open engine compartment. "Do you even know what you're looking for?"

She sucks a shivering breath through her teeth. I have a feeling it's just to delay her answer, which is, "Nope."

Cold, spidery panic crawls under my heart, but I

stomp it out before it gets to be anything more. Panicking is the worst thing I can do right now, right next to crying my eyes out. It won't get me closer to a solution.

I look down at the machinery, but I'm not really sure what I'm supposed to be seeing. There aren't any sparking wires or plumes of black smoke or anything that looks obviously dislodged.

Marisa would know what to do. She always did.

I squint up at Zahira through the rain. "Now what?"

She sighs through her nose and looks around as if there might be a brand-new engine lying on the side of the road. Another sigh, and she looks down the way we're supposed to be going. The highway goes on forever and ever.

"Okay," she finally says. "Okay. Hands out." I pull my arms back, and she shuts the engine hood. Very slowly, she says, "We are hitching a ride to the nearest exit, and then we are calling an auto shop."

She nods to herself like it's a great plan, which I guess it is, considering I can't think of a better one. I hug my arms against the cold and watch her stick her thumb out.

Hitchhiking is risky. That's why Marisa and I never did it. If the driver happens to be someone who watches the news, then it's game over for us. But I can't explain that to Zahira without also explaining that the cops are looking for me, so every time a car comes towards us, I stare straight at the driver and try to shoot a message through my eyes. *Don't stop. Don't stop. Don't stop.*

Three cars have passed, and none have slowed down. I know it's definitely not because of what I'm doing, but some part of me feels a little accomplished anyway.

What would Marisa do? We've never gotten stuck like this before. We *have* ditched our car-of-the-week on the side of long roads, though, and that's pretty much the same thing. We would walk, and that's what Zahira and I need to do right now.

I point to the road sign announcing the next exit. "How far is that?"

She glances over with a scowl, her thumb still stuck out. "Read it. Five kilos."

"I meant, how long is that going to take?"

She looks at me blankly for a second before she says, "Like, to *walk?*"

She says it like I asked her to kill a person.

"Unless you prefer standing here freezing your butt off in the rain," I say. "Nobody's stopping."

She makes a face like she ate something sour and blinks up at the sky. It's overcast, a little orange from city lights, and just like the highway, the clouds seem to go on forever and ever. It was only drizzling a moment ago, but now the raindrops are definitely getting bigger.

"Fine," she says after a big huff, and flings open the door to grab her stuff. "Five kilometers. That's, what, forty minutes? You can handle that?"

"I'm not a baby," I say. I've walked for longer with Marisa. I flip up my hood and pull on my backpack, and we begin our walk.

Five minutes later, I realize I made a mistake.

I'm supposed to take a painkiller with food. That's what the bottle says, and that's what Marisa always tells me, because otherwise it'll burn a hole through my stomach or whatever. But I didn't take one with my lunch because Zahira would have seen it and she would have asked "what is that?" and "are you hurt?" and yada yada yada, and I didn't want to deal with that. I thought I could make it till dinner, anyway. My side hurts, but it's more like a low burning. The kind of pain I can grit my teeth through.

Walking for five minutes makes it feel like my insides are ripping open.

I press a hand to my side through my hoodie pocket and pray that my guts won't fall apart. Is that where my spleen is? I wonder how long it'll take before it turns into runny-egg-sludge and leaks out. That's disgusting. I don't know why I thought of that.

Just keep going, Dany. You can do it. One foot in front of the other.

"Dany," Zahira says. My hearing is going all muffled, and she sounds far away.

"Yeah?" I say. It's not exactly freezing cold, but my breath comes out in a puff of white.

"Are you okay?"

I look up from the white painted line I've been following and realize Zahira doesn't just sound far away. She *is* far away. When did I lag so much? Raising my head makes me dizzy, so I stop walking.

"Fine," I call back, and wipe the wet, stringy hair out of my eyes. "Guess I'm just tired."

She gives me that *I don't believe you* look again. To prove her wrong, I start walking again. That makes the edges of my eyes turn black and my side throb like it's about to explode. But I must have been convincing enough because Zahira goes back to walking, too.

"I can't remember the last time I had to walk this much," she grumbles, adjusting her bag strap. "Didn't have much time for exercise in school. Campus was big, so sometimes it took ten minutes to get to my class. I think that's the most I did. Sometimes I had to run. *That* was a real workout."

I can tell she's just talking to fill up the space between the rustle of rain on leaves and passing cars, so I don't say anything and just focus on holding my gut together through willpower.

Zahira talks about school and coursework and annoying things that happened on campus, like the massive lineups at the bookstore at the start of school years, or the time they got a new cafeteria but the food was worse and somehow cost twice as much as before, or the absolute horror show that was waking up at 7 A.M. to register for courses before they all filled up. Somehow, I don't want her to stop talking. It feels like a lullaby, taking my mind away from the pain and the cold and the rain sogging up my socks. I guess some part of me is curious, too. About university and college life and all that. Marisa never talked about it. I've never seen movies about it. And I don't think I would ever get to live it.

Zahira talks and talks, and I try to picture it. Zahira walking around with her friends, carrying her heavy and expensive textbooks, hanging out with Aaron before he turned out to be a douchebag, smacking her alarm clock when her dorm is still dark so she can make her 8:00 A.M. classes. She said she was a med student. I wonder if she ever dissected any frogs.

We finally get to the bottom of the exit ramp, and Zahira asks the nearest store for the auto shop's phone number. I sit on the curb, hugging my stomach, and a few minutes later Zahira scrapes down beside me, holding her dialling phone to her ear. I half-heartedly listen to her talk to the auto person who picks up. Mostly I'm looking at a pool of shiny, rainbow oil on the wet asphalt.

"Seventy-five?" Zahira says. "Okay. And to fix it? Oh. Okay."

Seventy-five. That's a lot of money. It's money we can't afford to spend. How much did we take from Man #1 and Man #2? I don't think I ever asked Zahira. But her car breaking down definitely wasn't part of our budget.

"Okay," Zahira says, and explains where to pick us up. "Thank you." She hangs up the phone and gives a full-body sigh.

"Seventy-five is a lot," I say without really thinking. I feel like my brain turned to soup along with my spleen.

"And that's just for towing," she says, putting her phone away.

"How much is it to fix?"

"They said it depends on the problem. They're low on staff and low on parts."

"Do we have enough money?"

"I don't know."

"What if we don't?"

I hate how helpless I sound.

What would Marisa do?

The rain is picking up, slapping so hard on the asphalt it sounds like hail. The awning above the shop entrance protects us, but when the wind is strong I can feel a cold mist.

"We'll figure it out," Zahira says with a wrinkle between her eyebrows. "I just got to get my car in first. Can't leave her on the side of the road."

My brain says *yes we can* but my mouth says nothing because I just had the horrible realization that I made another mistake. What would Marisa do? She would not call the auto shop. She would not waste the money. She would take us to the nearest parking lot and pick a car and I would spark the lock and we would be back on our way and we wouldn't be here, sitting on the curb, waiting for the tow truck to come pick us up.

Zahira's phone rings again, and this time I try my hardest to hear the other end of the call. Tow Truck Guy's tinny voice says something like *we tried a jump start* and *didn't work* and *take a closer look in the shop* and *are you still in the same location?*

"Yes," Zahira says.

Tow Truck Guy says, *Perfect, we'll be there soon.*

"Ask him how long it'll take," I say.

Zahira scowls. "Huh?"

"Ask him," I say harder, "how long it'll take to fix your car."

She's still scowling, but she asks, "How long do you think it'll take to fix my car?"

The rain got bigger and now I can't hear what Tow Truck Guy is saying. But I can tell by Zahira's unchanging scowl that it isn't anything good.

"What did he say?" I ask the moment she hangs up.

"He *said,*" she says in a way that also doubles as *why the hell are you in such a rush,* "that he's not sure because he doesn't know what the problem is yet, but they will look at it tomorrow, and they will probably get it fixed in the next few days, depending on if they have the parts."

That might be the worst string of words I have ever heard. "Did you pay them already?"

She looks at me funny. "I can't pay over the phone."

Good. That's good. Then we haven't lost anything yet, except the time we spent sitting here doing nothing.

I stand up as quickly as I can without disturbing my side and say, "We have to go."

She stands too, bewildered. "Go *where?*"

There's a small parking lot across the street. I look both ways before I cross towards it.

"Dany, they're picking us up *here,*" she calls behind me.

"We're not waiting for them." I call back. I shouldn't be yelling. It draws attention.

"What? No! My *car!*"

"We don't need it."

She makes a sound like a cross between a choke and a laugh. "Of *course* we do."

I'm all the way across the street before she decides to run after me, as much as she can run in her heeled boots. There are twelve cars in the lot, and I don't know which one I'm supposed to pick. I don't know how Marisa picks. I should have paid attention.

Zahira clops to a stop beside me and says, a little out of breath, "Dany, what are you doing?"

I pick a blue minivan that looks new enough to not be in risk of problems but old enough that it won't stand out. I spark the lock and pop the door open, and Zahira actually gasps.

"*Dany,*" she hisses. "*What* are you *doing?*"

What am I doing? Isn't it obvious? This is our way out. No need to pay. No need to wait. But she just doesn't get it. She doesn't get that we can't waste the time and money and I don't know how to explain it to her. I have to get to Suddence. I don't know what I would do if I can't get there.

I spark open the panel under the steering wheel. I've seen Marisa hotwire cars before. I've seen it on TV. But when I pry the panel away and look into the compartment, there are too many wires and I don't know which ones I'm supposed to use. Marisa makes it look so easy, and she's not here and I don't know what to do. I don't know what to do.

Zahira pulls on my arm. "*Dany.*"

I want to fling her off. I want to snap at her—*let go!* If she can just stop bothering me, I can figure this out, and we'll be back on our way.

But suddenly I feel so tired and weak and lightheaded and *tired* and I can't get the words past my mouth. My chest is low and heavy, and hot tears are pushing their way up. I bury my face in my hands and try not to sob, but that makes it hard to breathe and I can't catch my breath and I just want to scatter away into nothing.

"Dany." I feel her hand on my shoulder. Her voice is soft now. She guides me out of the car and sits me down on the curb. I keep my face buried. I don't want her to look at me.

"Dany," she says again. "Tell me what the problem

is."

It's raining and cold but I feel all hot and sweaty. My hands are staticky fuzz, and I feel so, so weak. All I can say is "I need to get there."

"I'll get you there. I promise." She rubs my shoulder. "But not like this, okay? We don't need to go that far."

She says it like a hypothetical. Marisa and I have already gone that far.

I wish I could tell her everything. It's exhausting holding everything back.

"I can't wait a few days." My throat feels swollen and the words sound thick and wet. "I can't."

"Okay." Her teeth chatters as she sucks in a deep breath. "Okay. Let's just think about this, alright?" I hear her shift around to sit beside me. Her shoulder shudders against mine. I feel cold now, too, like all the heat left in a big rush and now I'm all clammy and shaky. "They're already towing my car. I have to pay them for that. We might be able afford the repairs, but then we'll lose the money we need for gas and motel and food." She huffs and rubs her shoulders. "And we lose a few days, and you can't wait that long."

She doesn't ask me why. That's a big relief.

"So." She thinks for a while, and then laughs. Just the sigh of a laugh. "Well. I do have an idea."

I sniff and scrape my hands up to my forehead. "What?"

"It's a last resort. You're not going to like it."

I sniff again. "Why?"

"It has to do with Aaron."

My head snaps up. "*No.*" I should have meant, *I don't*

want to get anyone else involved, but it's actually, "He's a douchebag."

She raises her eyebrows along with her shoulders. "We don't have a choice."

"Yes, we do. We take this car and we go."

"No. We're not stealing."

"And you said you didn't know where Aaron is. I heard you."

"Well. I lied."

That shocks me. Genuinely. "Why? He ditched you. He was going to let you get *kidnapped.*"

"Look, I hate his guts." She says *hate* like *haaaaate.* "But he lives with his brother now, and his brother is nice."

"You thought Aaron was nice."

"JJ is *actually* nice. And there's no way I'm getting him into trouble with those skeevy loan sharks. So I lied."

I still feel bitter about it, but it makes sense. I scrub my nose and stare across the lot. "So what's the plan?"

"I can call JJ. He lives maybe half an hour out. He can pick us up, we'll spend a night at his place, and then first thing tomorrow, we go. We borrow his car, and we go." She folds her arm atop her knees and glances down at me. "How does that sound?"

It sounds like getting *two* more people involved. Getting Zahira involved was bad enough. But she's right. We don't have a choice. I don't think I can last long like this.

"First thing tomorrow?" I say.

"Promise." She knocks her knee against mine. "And I promise I'll protect you from Aaron's douchebaggery."

That steals a laugh out of me. It comes so suddenly that I hiccup, and then Zahira's laughing, and I'm laughing even harder, through all the hiccups and the tears still in my eyes. For a scary moment I want to hug her, or I want her to hug me. But luckily, across the street, a tow truck rumbles in with Zahira's pink car.

"Come on," Zahira says, craning her neck that way. "I need to talk to him about my car. And then we can get the hell out of here."

Dear diary.

Marisa wants to say something. I can tell because she keeps taking an extra deep breath. But then she doesn't say anything and just keeps driving.

We've been going for three hours. Now we're going into a truck stop. Marisa tells me to turn around, and she wipes the cop's blood off my neck. I don't say thank you. Why would I. She's mad at me anyway.

She says, "I'll get you some food and water. Stay here."

I stay because there's nowhere else I can go.

She comes back with energy bars and water.

I'm so hungry. I know I'm eating the energy bars too fast, but I can't help it.

And she's doing it again. Taking a deep breath like she wants to say something, and then changing her mind. It's so annoying. Just spit it out.

She says, "We need to talk about the sparks."

I don't know what she wants me to say. I just ignore her and drink some water.

And she's doing it AGAIN. Taking a breath. Changing her mind. I say, "What?"

She takes a long time to say, "You need to be careful."

I have to be careful? She's the one who went out and broke our cardinal rules.

She says, "Your sparks aren't supposed to be visible. It could have been dangerous back there."

I say, "I was trying to protect us."

She says, "I know, but..." She's thinking about how to put it. "Your powers are growing. Even faster than I thought. And I don't know how much more it will grow. I just...I don't want it to get to a point where you can't control it."

What is she talking about? Did she not see what I did? I say, "I CAN control it."

She still doesn't believe me. I can tell.

I say, "I CAN. You SAW me."

She says, "You can. For now."

She makes me so mad. Those were the biggest sparks I ever made. Nobody got hurt. SHE was the one who shot somebody. None of it was my fault. I didn't get caught because They happened to see me. The cops were ALREADY THERE. The motel owner CALLED THEM because she recognized BOTH OF US. It's not because I got careless, but Marisa is making it all about ME, how I should have somehow done better, as if my power is some super radioactive bomb that should never be used, as if my power didn't SAVE us, and all this time SHE was the one who went out to meet one of our goddamn enemies.

I say, "Why did you meet Lilian?"

She looks surprised. "How did you know that?"

I say, "I heard you. You lied to me. You said you wouldn't call her anymore. Why did you meet her? You said we were supposed to stay away from anyone from the clinic. That includes her! You keep telling me everyone at the clinic is bad, but you never include her, and I don't get it!"

She says, "It doesn't matter!"

I say, "It does! It matters because this is my life too! It's my life and you don't get to not tell me things! It's not fair!"

I'm yelling. I know I shouldn't be, but I don't care. I'm just so angry. Marisa doesn't argue back. She just puts her hands on the steering wheel and closes her eyes.

She says, "It doesn't matter because it was a lie. It was all a lie. She said whatever she needed to get me away from you, and that's how the cops knew when to catch you alone. She was part of it. I know she was."

She looks so sad that I can't be mad at her anymore, and I'm even madder at myself for forgiving her so easily. I stare at the gas station price sign and try hard not to cry.

It's not working.

Marisa says, "I'm sorry. I shouldn't have left you alone. I should have known better."

Yeah, you should've.

I hear her turning in her seat to face me. She says, "Dany. What do I have to do? How do I make it up for you?"

I spin around and say, "Promise you'll never do anything stupid like that again."

She nods and says, "I won't. I promise."

"And never, EVER lie to me again."

"I won't."

That's it. But it doesn't sound like enough.

"And you owe me two ice creams now."

And then we're both laughing even though I'm still crying, and she hugs me. Somewhere deep deep down I'm still mad at her, but for now, all I care about is how much I don't want to let go.

PART III:
Leave No Trace

AARON'S BROTHER JJ arrives in a blue, wood-panelled station wagon, and he's not at all what I was expecting.

I guess I was picturing a businessman. Suit and tie and the whole shebang. When Zahira was calling him, she said she wasn't sure if he would pick up because he has a job. I didn't ask what job. I just thought it was a businessman job.

JJ isn't dressed like a businessman. He has a pilled-up hoodie over a tank top with a bowl of noodles printed on it and greyed jeans like mine. His black curly hair is as long as mine used to be, and he has messy stubbles.

He pulls to a rocky stop, his window already rolled down despite the rain pelting down in sheets, and says, "Zahira!"

"JJ!" Zahira had brightened the moment she saw JJ's car, and now, as she says his name like a celebration, she's absolutely beaming. They hug through the open window, and I just stand beside Zahira's luggage, not knowing what to do.

When they finally break apart, Zahira points at me with her thumb. "Dany. Family friend's kid."

"Hi!" JJ sticks his hand out the window. He just oozes enthusiasm. No, *ooze* is too slow. He's like if you poked holes in a water balloon and squeezed.

I don't like shaking people's hands because there's always a chance their hand will be hot and sticky and gross. Thankfully, JJ's hand is dry.

"Hop in!" he says. "Get out of the rain!"

We shove Zahira's luggage in the trunk and pile into his car, Zahira in the front, me in the back with the tools and trash. I have to maneuver a hard hat out of the way so my legs have somewhere to go.

"Sorry about the mess," JJ says as he pulls onto the street. "I fix things."

"You *tinker*," Zahira says, pulling on her seatbelt.

"No, no, I *fix*. That oven I found last time? Fixed."

"Did you test it?"

"Yes."

"And it *didn't* explode?"

Oh, great, so I have to be their third wheel. As if I couldn't be any more miserable. The pain in my side is a little less horrible now, but it still hurts more than it did yesterday. If it was just the pain, it wouldn't be so annoying. But it's not. It's making me nauseous. Today I almost couldn't finish my lunch. And it feels like there's a layer of glass between me and my brain, and I know I should be pounding on it and trying to break it down but I just...don't really want to.

I should have taken the painkiller this morning.

"So, Dany," JJ says, positively beaming at me through the rear-view mirror. "How old are you?"

"Eleven."

"What school do you go to?"

"I'm homeschooled." That's the practiced answer. I'm supposed to say that to anyone who asks. It's not really a lie, anyway.

"Cool! Where are you going with Zahira, anyway?"

"My house," Zahira says. "Dany's been, like, dying to see Poquito."

I don't know *what* Poquito is, but going by the excited gasp JJ just released, it must be a very, very believable lie. I had my own made-up story ready, but since Zahira's is obviously so much better, I just nod and make my lips smile.

"What about your parents?" JJ asks. "They don't want to see little Poquito?"

"They're allergic," Zahira says smoothly.

I think maybe grownups are better at lying.

The rest of the car ride is just the smooth *ba-bumps* of the road and the radio blasting local commercials. It all makes me want to fall asleep. I don't want to though, so I wrestle my eyes open and count all the green cars we see instead.

My fingers wander to the bump in my hoodie, where the key hangs around my neck. I try to feel the patterns of the rubber cover, the colourful design and the bright, bubbly number. It had felt so heavy yesterday when I thought I wouldn't reach Suddence in time.

I clutch it tight through my clothes, relief working slowly through my body.

I haven't failed. I'm on my way.

We finally pull onto the slope of an underground parking garage. JJ parks, and I drag myself out of the car, groaning when Zahira orders me to carry one of her wheeled suitcases. We lug all her stuff to the elevator, and on the way up, JJ and Zahira discuss dinner, debating whether to order out or heat up some leftovers, and I have to hold my side through my pocket again because my spleen feels in real danger of liquefying. I already have a plan in my head: the moment we get into JJ's apartment, I'll announce that I need to pee, and then I'll go to the washroom and drink as much water as I can handle and take a painkiller. There's no way I can wait until dinner.

The elevator crawls up at the speed of whatever the hell crawls slowly.

Ding! Ground floor.

Ding! Second floor.

Ding! Third floor.

Ding! Fourth floor.

The doors slide open on the fifth floor, and JJ leads us to his apartment room. He slides his key into the lock, and I'm about to breathe out in relief, except his hand freaking freezes and he turns to Zahira with a face that's all squinty-eyed and pressed lips. It's a look that says *There's something I didn't tell you.*

"There's something I didn't tell you," he says.

Zahira frowns. "What?"

Like a secret, JJ admits, "I didn't tell Aaron you were coming."

"Oh, good. Then maybe when he sees me, he'll have a heart attack and die."

And I want to say *Oh, good, then maybe we can go inside if this conversation is over.*

"Actually," Zahira says, "there's something I have to tell you, too."

I give Zahira dagger eyes, but I don't think she notices.

"I kind of promised my parents I would be there by tomorrow, so I was wondering if I could borrow your car for a day or so? Just to drop Dany off at my parents' place, and then I'll bring it right back."

JJ makes an ungodly long "Hmmmmmmmmmm…"

"Pretty please?"

JJ makes a higher, impossibly longer "*Hmmmmmmmmmmmmmmmmmmm…*"

"Can you guys talk about this inside?" I say loudly. "I need to pee."

JJ unlocks the door with an "Oh, yes!" and points me towards the bathroom. The door is locked, though, which can only mean one thing: that rat-fuck son of a bitch Aaron is inside.

"Aaron, you in there?" JJ asks, even though it's obvious.

"Yeah," he calls from the other side.

"We have visitors."

The toilet flushes, and Aaron comes out saying, "Sorry, if I knew people were coming, I would have…" But then he sees Zahira and flinches back with a "Jesus *Christ.*"

Zahira crosses her arms and leans back, all steely-eyed and cool, but as much as I would love to see how she mangles Aaron, I have more important things to care about.

I slip past the douchebag and shut myself in the

bathroom. Marisa always tells me not to drink straight from the faucet because we have no idea how clean their pipes are, but I don't care anymore. I fill my cupped hands with as much water as I can and chug it all down and swallow a pill with another handful of water. It'll take a bit before the medicine kicks in, but the relief hits me now. Feathery, cold-sweat relief.

I check the bottle. Only two pills left.

It's okay, Dany. You just have to last one more day.

Outside, I can hear Aaron and Zahira whisper-arguing. I'm not sure I can handle that until the medicine completely kicks in.

I scrub my hands clean with soap and check my bandages. It hasn't bled through. It can probably last until I take a shower later.

I take a quick inventory of my stuff and put out what I'll need later. Toothbrush and toothpaste. Tiny bottle of shampoo because I don't trust the bar of crusty soap JJ has sitting on the side of his splotchy bathtub. Towel—no. I'll keep that in my bag for now. JJ's towel bar doesn't look like it can handle anything more than a tissue paper.

Aaron and Zahira are *still* arguing, but I don't want to be in the bathroom anymore, so I come out as loudly as I can, hoping they'd hear me and stop fighting. But even with how much I made the hinges squeak and how hard I slapped the light switch, they're still sniping away.

I peek into the living room. JJ is standing by the TV, one finger on his lip like he's wondering how to break up the fight, and Aaron and Zahira are smack in the middle of the room. Center-stage for the angriest performances of all time.

"—the more and more I thought about it, the more scared I got," Aaron is saying. He reminds me of a bird. Big round eyes like an owl, long sharp nose like a beak, bleached white hair going in every direction like duckling tufts. "I just—I didn't—"

"*I was scared too,*" Zahira spits through her teeth. "Did that ever occur to you? Did that thought ever get through that stupid thick skull?"

Aaron flattens his hands together and touches them to his lips for a second, like he's slipping in a speed prayer. "I'll make it up to you," he promises, and he sounds so…what's the word…earnest? And his big eyes are sparkling like a kitten begging for milk. For a second I seriously thought about forgiving him.

Get it together, Dany. Don't make it so easy.

"I'll make it up to you," he says again because Zahira only scoffed and rolled her head back. "I will. Just—just tell me what I need to do."

"Nothing!" Zahira says, snapping her head forward again. "Nothing you do will ever make up for the *shit* you put me through. You—"

And then she sees me lurking around the corner, and she sucks back whatever she was going to say. Aaron follows her eyes and turns around. I give him a *look* that makes it perfectly clear we're not going to be friends.

"Can we talk about this more later?" Aaron asks. *Pleads.*

Zahira gives him a stare that is all knives.

"Zahira."

He doesn't get an answer, so he just leaves with a deep, deep sigh. But not before giving me a strange look, like he's just now realizing he has no idea who I am.

Once the bedroom door closes, Zahira plants her hands on her hips and breathes out all the air from her lungs.

"I'll go make some tea," JJ says.

"And I need to take a piss," Zahira seethes.

She breezes past me, and from the redness in her eyes, I get the feeling that's not the real reason she wants to go to the bathroom.

JJ and I are alone now. I didn't realize how much space Zahira's anger was taking up until now that she's gone. Suddenly the living room is extremely quiet and a few degrees colder.

"Well," JJ says. "Take a seat. I'll be right back."

He disappears into the kitchen.

I look for a place to sit down, but JJ is a slob, alright. The mess in his car is nothing compared to his living room. It's easier to describe what *isn't* covered by cups and crusty bowls and magazines and envelopes and some kind of paperwork. A corner of the sofa where I guess JJ usually sits. A few spots on the carpet just big enough to step on. A section in the middle of the wooden coffee table that looks conspicuously empty. I bet the things that used to be there are what JJ is clattering around in the kitchen right now.

None of the sofas look safe to sit on, so I pick my way carefully through the mess to inspect the room instead. Even the *walls* are covered in stuff, shelves and pictures and posters for some band I've never heard of. I don't understand how one person can have so much stuff. All my things fit in my backpack and the yellow suitcase that got confiscated by the cops. Even when Marisa and I lived in our townhouse, it never got to be this messed up.

I stop by a DVD tower and peek at the titles. I recognize a few movie names, but none of them look official. They're all in cheap plastic cases with covers that are very obviously printed at home, all pixelly and slightly off-colour.

"You like movies?" JJ calls from the kitchen door, drying a tea cup.

I nod.

"You can pick one to watch. I'll pop it in for you."

I turn back to the DVDs and scan the titles more thoroughly. I almost gasp when I see a familiar one in its iconic bright yellow font.

In the kitchen, JJ puts a kettle on the burner and comes out to join me. I pull the DVD from the stack and suddenly feel embarrassed. Most of the movies in the tower are action movies, and I picked out one about high school and singing and basketball.

But when JJ takes it, his grin is so big I can see 80% of his teeth. "Oh, yeah," he says, smacking the DVD against his palm and heading for the TV. "Hey, Zahira, you better come out! It's throwback time!"

He pops it into the player under the TV, which I can't help but notice is super old. Like, *ancient* old. It makes me wonder if he picked it out of someone's trash and fixed it just for fun.

The movie starts, and I frown, realizing that even though they play the movie on TV a lot, I've never actually seen the beginning. I don't even know the opening song.

But clearly Zahira does, because the moment the first note plays, she busts out of the bathroom.

"You can't watch that without me," she says.

JJ grins. "You two watch it. I'll go get the tea."

"Sit," Zahira tells me, clearing out a spot on the sofa. I set my backpack down and curl up. Zahira doesn't look so mad anymore. I glance at the bedroom, where Aaron disappeared into, but the door is closed, and I don't think he'll be coming out anytime soon.

JJ comes back with a tray of teacups and passes them out. I take a sip of the reddish tea. It's spicy. Well, *spicey,* like it has a lot of spices in it.

"Like it?" JJ asks, and I nod. "There's more in the kitchen if you want a refill."

"Thank you," I say, and cringe at how stiff and proper I sound. I take a big slurp of tea to make up for it.

The second song of the movie starts playing, and Zahira and JJ sing along at the top of their lungs. I know *this* song, but I don't want to sing out loud, so I just hum. It's weird seeing Zahira and JJ like this. They're grownups. Marisa doesn't seem that much older than them, but I can't picture her singing along to this movie. I can't picture her hanging out at a friend's house. I can't picture her laughing. Not like this. She's always been serious, even before we went on the run. I know it's because of me. Because she has to care for me. Watch out for me. Worry about me.

If we made it out of the country, would we laugh like this, too?

JJ gets a lyric wrong. Zahira laughs, and when the next chorus comes, she purposely gets it wrong too, and

JJ smacks her with a pillow. When the next song plays, I sing a little under my breath, and the next song, I sing louder.

I want to stay here forever. After I reach Suddence, there won't be times like this anymore.

But for now, I can let myself believe this has always been my life.

Dear diary.

We slept in the car last night. Marisa let me have the backseat and she slept sitting up in the driver's seat. It was cold. The radio said it'll be negative degrees for the next few days. It might even snow. The weather lady said it all chipper, like it's something to be excited about.

We can't leave the heater on or it'll drain the car battery or something, so we just put on as much clothes as we could, but I still shivered the whole night. I didn't sleep very much.

Marisa found a mall parking lot that had a few of those big camper vans parked inside and decided it was safe enough. At least we know we won't get kicked out because they obviously let people stay in the lot overnight.

I remember once I tried to get Marisa to buy

a camper van. Then we wouldn't have to keep spending money on motels, and it looks soooo much more comfortable than a car. But Marisa said it wouldn't work out "logistically" (I don't know what that means) because:

1) it's big and recognizable

2) it's clunky and slow

Still though, I thought it would be nice to try one, at least for one day. Maybe Marisa will change her mind when this is over and the cops are on lower alert. Whenever the heck THAT happens.

It's about 7 o'clock now. Marisa and I are going back to the mall washroom to clean up a little. We tried going last night, but it was closed because it was almost midnight.

I didn't brush my teeth last night, and when I woke up this morning I felt so grimy. My mouth was stinky. We didn't shower last night either. My WHOLE BODY is extra smelly and crusty. The best we can do right now is wash our faces in the mall washroom. Wiping my face with the brown paper towel is probably one of the worst experiences I ever had. It's so...well, papery. And it smells weird, like I shouldn't be putting it anywhere near my face.

I shouldn't complain. I keep telling myself

that. I should be glad we're both still free and alive. But I can't help it, okay? I keep feeling so mad, and I want to punch something, or at least bite something really hard.

I'm in the washroom stall, and I can hear Marisa taking something out of her bag. Usually I hate when washroom doors have really big gaps, but it's a good thing this time because it means I can spy on Marisa. She's like a different person when she thinks I can't see her. Her whole face suddenly turns all deep and dark. She's looking at her medicine bottle, and I can tell it's empty. She throws the bottle away as quietly as possible. If I wasn't spying, I don't think I would have heard it at all.

How long has the bottle been empty? Did she take her medicine yesterday? She never told me what it's for. She never told me she takes medicine, period. I could ask. She promised me she would never lie to me again. But I'm scared to find out the answer. What happens if she stops taking the medicine? ~~Would she die?~~

I come out of the stall. Marisa is putting on an orange reflective vest. It means we're about to rob some vending machines.

It's still very early, so none of the shops are open, and there's barely anybody in the mall. We find two vending machines. There are a few old people loitering. I guess it's too cold to take walks outside, so they're walking in the mall.

Me and Marisa have a system worked out though, and it's one we used in places that are even more crowded than this. Since she's wearing the orange vest, nobody would think she's suspicious. She's just a worker. But if a kid starts hanging out with her while she's opening up the machines, THAT becomes suspicious. So I find a bench a good few shops down, and Marisa goes to the machine that sells drinks first. She crouches down and pretends to unlock the coin box with a key. I spark the lock, and the box pops open. She collects the money inside. None of the old people look at her.

Then I have to change my position so I can see the vending machine that sells food. Same process. Pretend to unlock, spark the box, take money. No one will be able to tell the machines are broken until the mall opens for real, and by then we'll be gone. And it's not like They would hear about this and go "vending machine vandalism? Must be Dany and Marisa!" They probably wouldn't hear about it at all. The cops would, though, so doing this always makes me feel like we're about to get caught. Marisa always says the key to not getting caught is to not act suspicious. Stop looking over my shoulder and stop tensing up and definitely don't run. I try my best. But what if Marisa trips and all the money falls out of her pockets? I don't think any amount of not acting suspicious would get us out of that.

We head back to the car separately, me first. Marisa catches up to me halfway across the lot and leads me to a different car. Spark the lock. Hot wire the engine. Back on our way. To where? I don't even know anymore.

She gives me the money and I count it. There's a little more than a hundred. Enough for a few days, at least. She got all the change, too, and I look for some special coins, and I get hit with this weird heavy panicky feeling that this is going to be the rest of my life. Always driving. Always stealing. I try to picture myself doing this when I'm seventeen. When I'm twenty-five. When I'm thirty. I can't do it. The same way I can't imagine Marisa as a kid. One day I'm going to be the same age as Marisa. Will I still be doing this? Will we still be running? Do we even have a chance of making it out of the country?

Thinking about it is making me even more panicky, so I just count the coins and show Marisa a special one because maybe that would make this feel normal. Like she's just my regular mom and I'm just a regular kid and all I have to worry about is if I can find a special coin I've never seen before.

My shoe is falling apart.

I don't want this to be forever.

I DIDN'T MEAN to fall asleep in the middle of my favourite movie. But the next thing I know, I'm waking up and it's 7:43 P.M. and the credits are playing. Zahira and JJ are moving pots and pans around in the kitchen, still singing songs from the movie. I can't remember the last part I saw before I passed out. Was it when the team lost their first game?

I don't want to be alone, so I join Zahira and JJ in the kitchen.

"Ah, the sleepy beauty awakes!" JJ says.

"It's *sleeping* beauty," says Zahira, holding a large oven tray.

"*Whaaat*ever."

The pain in my side is cold and faraway because of the medicine, but I still feel a little weak. Like even without the pain, my body knows I shouldn't be standing up. I don't want to go back to the living room though, so I sit on a stepping stool that nobody is using and watch Zahira and JJ do whatever it is they're doing.

"Are you making dinner?" I ask. I'm not hungry. I

just want to know.

"*I'm* making dinner," JJ says, firing up the stove. "*Zahira* is making something for me."

Zahira rolls her eyes. But it's a nice roll this time. I'm not sure how that's possible. "It's for *everyone.*"

"No. All of them. For me."

I watch Zahira roll out a box of pre-made pastry and ask, "What are you making?"

"Baklava."

I don't know what that is. But going by the buttery liquid and the bowl of what smells like sugar syrup beside the pan, it has to be good. "What's that?"

"Dessert. You're not allergic to anything, are you?"

I shake my head.

"Good." She rummages in the drawers for a brush. "This is going to be lesser baklava because I don't have all the ingredients." She finds a rubbery-looking brush and begins streaking the dry pastry with the buttery liquid. "Like, this isn't even the right type of pastry."

Zahira and JJ start a whole debate over whether the pastry type matters. When I hear hinges creak, I peek around the kitchen doorway.

Aaron is casing the joint through the cracked-open bedroom door. When he sees that we're all busy in the kitchen, he slips out and snatches a mug of coffee off the living room table. Everything about him is sharp, especially since the living room lights are off and the TV is casting this ghastly pale glow on everything. It seems like all his bones are trying to eject from his body.

He sees me spying, and I give him a hard stare.

"D-A-N-I Dani," Zahira sings, like it's a commercial

jingle, and I turn back to the kitchen. "Did you hear anything we just said?"

"That's not how you spell my name," I say.

"What is it, then?"

"D-A-N-Y."

"Aren't you missing an N in there?" JJ calls over the whir of the stove hood.

"No," I say. "You wouldn't get it."

"Well, JJ was saying that he has a date tomorrow morning."

"At the movie theater!" he interjects.

Zahira does that eyeroll again. "He needs the car for it, but because he's such a good friend, he promised to be back by noon, and we can have the car."

"Oh," I say. I try to do the math. We would be in Ornament City just before dinnertime. That's acceptable.

"I'm sacrificing quality hangout time for you guys, man," JJ complains, though he doesn't actually sound upset.

"And I'm making baklava to make up for it, aren't I?"

They sound like they've already had this argument. Well, *argument* doesn't seem like the right word. It's a *nice* argument, like Zahira's nice eyeroll.

In the living room, the movie music suddenly ends, and there's the sound of Aaron flipping through the cable channels.

In a low voice, Zahira says, "Ugh, is that Aaron?"

I glance around the corner even though I already know it is. "Yup."

"Can you grab something for me?"

I make a face. "What?"

"In the entryway, where we dropped everything—remember that little dog statue I got?"

I squint a little and nod. How could I possibly forget.

"Can you go grab it? I need to show it to JJ."

I make a sound between a sigh and a groan and slink off the stepping stool, but secretly, I'm celebrating my luck. If *I'm* the one who goes to get the weird dog statue, then I'll have the chance to throw away the newspaper wrapped around it before Zahira ever sees it.

The entryway has a direct view of the living room, which I'm 100% sure is the reason Zahira told *me* to get the statue. She just can't bear to even be in Aaron's line of sight. His eyes are glued on the TV screen though, and when I sneak out of the kitchen, he doesn't seem to notice me.

I kick around the luggage until I find the bag of thrifted goods. I crumple up the newspaper and shove it in my pocket before bringing the statue back to the kitchen.

"Oh my god!" JJ exclaims when he sees it. "It *does* look just like Poquito!"

"See? I told you," Zahira says with victory.

I look down at the statue. So this Poquito they speak of is a dog.

And then Zahira's joy suddenly vanishes, and I realize Aaron is at the doorway. Not entirely, though. Just his head and a bit of his shoulder, like there's radiation in the kitchen and he's afraid to fully expose himself to it.

"Zahira," he says.

Turning away, Zahira resumes her task of smashing

a plastic bag of almonds and pistachios with a rolling pin.

"Zahira," he presses, and I'm surprised he has the balls to speak again. "We need to talk."

I give him a look that says *get lost,* but he's too busy looking at Zahira, who's trying very hard not to look at him. JJ glances up from the stovetop, his eyes darting between the two of them like it's a very interesting tennis match.

"*Zahira.*"

She brings the rolling pin down with such a big *BANG!* that I have to make sure she didn't explode the whole bag of nuts. "*What?*" she says without turning around.

"We *have* to talk."

I don't know what's giving him so much confidence all of a sudden. Zahira spins around, her eyes nuclear. "Talk about what?"

"Not here," he whispers, as if then JJ and I wouldn't be able to hear it. He shifts impatiently. "Come on. *Please.*"

That seems to finally get Zahira. She growls under her breath but follows Aaron to the living room.

The kitchen feels weirdly empty without her. I don't know what to do, standing by the door with a ceramic dog statue, so I hover beside JJ and watch him cook up a simple meal of oily-green vegetables and a big steaming pot of rice that smells impossibly good. He heats up another pan and pours in a tub of leftover chicken. It looks like it's been in the tub for a while, but even that gets my mouth all watering.

When was the last time I had a proper hot meal? All

I had today was that cold wrap and orange juice. Yesterday I had fries and Zahira's hashbrown. The last truly hot meal I ate were those microwaved frozen burgers, and I'm not sure those even count.

The oven makes a beeping sound.

JJ mutters under his breath as he dishes out the food. "Go get Zahira," he tells me. "She has to put the stuff in the oven."

Yeah, and she has to actually *finish* making the stuff first.

I put the ceramic statue on the counter and trudge out of the kitchen. I was expecting Zahira to be in another whisper-fight with Aaron, but they're both silent in the blue-washed living room, Aaron sitting, Zahira standing, staring shocked at the TV.

Then their eyes slide slowly to me.

The TV volume is on low, still audible, but the news anchor's garble is static in my ears. I don't want to see what's on the screen. Maybe if I don't see it, then it isn't there, and this isn't happening.

But I force my head to turn. I force myself to look at the screen. At the newscast. At the blown-up high school. At the photo of Marisa.

At the photo of me.

Just like the weather lady said, it's even colder tonight. Luckily, we find a blanket in the trunk, and the car is big enough that when we put down the back seats, we get a space where we can lie down together and huddle.

I don't like sleeping in cars, but we're lucky to have it. Marisa says it's too risky to go to motels now, or even homeless shelters. The cops know we're in the area. Those are the places they'll look first. We've slept on the streets a couple times before, but that was when we still had all our stuff, and it was summer. If we tried that now, we would both be frozen tomorrow.

We parked under an overpass and called it an early night and went to sleep at 9pm, but I'm not asleep yet. I'm trying not to shiver. Maybe that would convince my body that I'm not cold.

But I can't help it. And every time a car passes above us, the *whoooosh* jars me back awake. I don't know how I can fall asleep like this.

Marisa is shivering even harder. I don't think it's just the cold. Her skin is looking weird, all pale and blotchy. And despite all the shivering, she's hot and sweaty. It's because she ran out of medicine. I know it is. But she's pretending like everything's fine, even though she's clearly running some kind of fever.

I can tell she's not asleep yet, either, so I say, "You promised you wouldn't lie to me again, right?"

She mumbles, "Mm-hm."

"What's that medicine you take?"

She's quiet for a while, like she's trying to comprehend it. She sighs and says, "You weren't supposed to know about it."

That's not an answer, so I say, "Well, YOU know everything about ME." That's not true. But right now I don't really care.

She still doesn't give me an answer, and I can't help but hate her a little.

I say, "When you make a promise, you're supposed to keep it."

She says, "I know." Quietly. So quietly I almost can't hear her. I huff and wrap my arms tighter. It's annoying because technically she ISN'T breaking the promise. She promised she wouldn't lie again, and she can't lie if she's not saying anything at all. Such a stupid loophole.

I say, "Fine. You don't have to answer that." But I do want at least SOMETHING answered tonight. I dig through my brain and think of Lilian. I want to know if they knew each other before the clinic. I want to know why she keeps calling Lilian, or why Lilian keeps calling her. They're supposed to be enemies. I know she would just say I wouldn't get it. It's a grownup thing. But still, I ask, "Did you know Lilian? Before the clinic?"

She sighs. I feel the heave and sag through our pressed-together backs. At first I think she might just brush it off again. But she says, "I knew her for a long time. We were friends."

"Is that it?" I wonder what it's like to have friends. I don't know if Marisa counts as a friend. I tell people she's my mom, but she isn't really. Do Lory and them count? I don't think so. They probably haven't even thought about me since I left.

Marisa says, "When I was about the same age as you, maybe two or three years older, I met her. We were at the grand opening for the little town my parents moved us to. The mayor was giving a speech. I saw her yawning and I said 'I think this is boring too' and she said 'I had to see this speech a thousand times.' The mayor was her mum. I was surprised because she didn't act like it. She was so nice and funny. But she only stayed there for the first year. Her mum wanted her to go to private school, so she went."

I ask, "What's private school?" It sounds like homeschooling, like what I did with Marisa, but it must be something different.

She says, "You dress all fancy. You pay more to get in."

I say, "That doesn't sound fun."

"She seemed to like it." I can almost hear a smile. "But we found ways to keep in touch. We would write letters, or we would call, and when I finally got a cellphone, we talked to each other all the time. My mum, she didn't like it. She said we were racking up the phone bill."

I can't imagine Marisa with a mom, or with a best friend. For my whole life it's always been just me and her. It's wrong, but I feel a little bitter. She had other people. I never did.

I turn the next question around in my head. I want to see if I'm right, if her being friends with Lilian is the reason she found Doctor Heed so quickly after my incident in school. But she sounds so calm right now, so happy, and this is the first time she's talking about her childhood. I want to hear more.

I say, "Could you have gone with her?"

Her hair scrubs against the carpeted ground as she shakes her head, just a little. "My parents wanted me to stay. They wanted to save the money. The school I went to was paid for by the town. And I didn't want to go, anyway. I liked living there. I still have the key. The little pink one, you know?"

I know what she's talking about. I've seen it on her keyring, bright and bubbly and totally not like Marisa at all, but I never asked what it's for. I knew she wouldn't tell me.

I try to imagine this town, but all I can think of is sunshine and rows of townhouses that look like the one we used to live in. I say, "Where's the town?"

"It's a very small town. You haven't heard of it."

"I want to know."

She's quiet for a while. I listen to her take a deep, deep breath, and I think she might not want to answer, but I can hear a smile when she says, "Suddence. A little town in the middle of nowhere, deep inside Ornament County."

She's right. I have never heard of it. I say, "Do you miss it?"

She laughs. It's a soft breath, smooth and feathery. "I do."

"Maybe we could go there. And live there." I try to remember what it was like living in a normal house. Having normal dinner and normal school and normal conversations. It seems like a different life. Not mine, like I'm seeing it in a show on TV. It's strange. We've only been on the run for two years, but somehow it feels like this has been my whole life. "You said it's a small town. Maybe they won't know who we are."

She goes all still. I can't see her face, but I can picture her smile disappearing. I can feel her happiness drain away like water turned cold.

She says very quietly, "We can't go back."

"Why?"

But instead of answering, she says, "You're from there too, you know."

I crane my neck and frown at her over the corner of my eye. "Really?"

"Really."

"How come you never told me?"

"I don't know," she says. "I guess I didn't think it mattered."

Of COURSE it matters. I never really thought about where I came from, but that was because this whole time I thought Marisa just picked me randomly from the orphanage.

I say, "Is that why you adopted me? Because we were from the same town?"

"Mm-hm."

I lie back and try to wrap my head around all of it. "Did you know my parents?"

"No."

"You're telling the truth this time, right?"

I hear her shifting around to look at me. "Dany, why would I lie to you?"

Before I lose my courage, I say, "Did you find Doctor Heed so quickly because of Lilian? Because she works for him?"

She lingers for a long time, and I can tell she's trying to think of a way to answer that proves she didn't lie to me, but in the end, she settles back down and says, "Yes." Quiet again, this time with shame. "Doctor Heed is her father. She introduced me to him."

So I was right. A tear prickles the corner of my eye, and I scrub it away. There's no use feeling betrayed, Dany. It's not like the truth changes anything. It doesn't change the fact we're here, or the fact Doctor Heed is after us, or the fact we will probably never, ever stop running away.

I just don't understand why she kept so much from me. If it made no difference in the end, why didn't she just tell me?

"Dany." Marisa is moving, turning around to face me, and I turn around too, blinking back my tears. Her face is all stern, but I see tears in her eyes, too. "Dany, I'm sorry. I shouldn't have lied to you. I was so scared. I didn't know how to explain it all. But I promised, right? I promised I wouldn't lie to you anymore."

I nod, a tear slipping down the side of my face.

"None of it changes this. They are still after us, and we can't let Them catch us, and I don't want you to think you can't trust me, alright? Anything you want to know, I will tell you."

I nod again and take a breath. It's supposed to be steadying, but it's shaky. "Why did you meet with her?" I hold her eyes. She's serious, and I need her to know I'm serious, too. "You say They're after us, and They're dangerous, but you keep calling her, and then you went to meet with her. Why?"

It's a heavy question. I can see the weight it has on Marisa. The serious light in her eyes dissolves into something faraway. Sadness.

"She said she had a way to get us out."

I frown a little. "And you believed her?"

"This isn't the first time she said it. She's been telling me her plan for a few months. She says she changed her mind, and she doesn't agree with her father anymore, and she wants to help. And this time, this time she said the plan needs to happen soon, and she needs to know if I was in. I was out of medicine. I was desperate. I took a chance." She closes her eyes and turns away, sinking onto her back. "And some part of me thought we might still be friends."

After a while, I say, "Do you really think she's lying?"

"Of course she was."

She doesn't sound so sure.

I watch the tears under her lashes, and the wax-like shine of her pale skin. Out of medicine.

"We could get more," I say. "More medicine. And then you'll be okay, right?"

"No more talking," she says, her eyes still closed. "Try to sleep. Tomorrow, we have a long way to go."

"TURN IT OFF." Zahira says it so quietly it makes me scared. I'm not sure what of. Just scared.

I guess it scares Aaron too because he does as he's told. His big owl eyes are on me. So are Zahira's, even as she goes to turn on the lights. My stare is glued to the screen. The TV is off now, but the headline is seared into my brain.

One body identified.

Marisa Lane.

The news anchor was saying no other bodies have been identified yet. But after a thorough search of the wreckage, there are no signs of the child Lane had abducted.

And there is no doubt Zahira and Aaron saw much, much more than that.

For a long time, Zahira just *looks* at me. Just *looks*. It's a look that says *Why the hell didn't you tell me?*

I say, "I thought you knew."

Oh. That's not convincing at all.

"You lied to me," she says, her anger steeping. "You

said nobody was after you."

"I didn't say that."

"You said you were *safe*. You said I didn't need to *worry*. Dany, this whole time, you didn't tell me every cop in the country is looking for you."

"I didn't think it mattered." And it shouldn't have mattered. Because if everything went according to plan, if the car hadn't broken down, we wouldn't be here. Zahira would never see this news, and by the time she realized who I am, she would have already dropped me off, and I would already be in Suddence and long, long gone.

"Doesn't *matter?*" Her voice hooks up violently, and she has to wrestle it down before JJ comes barging in asking what's wrong. "You think the fact that the *cops* are actively looking for you *doesn't matter?*"

"Okay, well, you know now, so what are you going to do about it?" I snap. "Nothing! You can't do anything! There was no point telling you! You would have just gotten scared and run away!"

She growls and clutches the sides of her face, like there's too much she wants to scream at me and she wishes she could just claw the words out and hurl them.

I don't have time for this.

I stomp over to my backpack and snatch it up. I was stupid enough to unpack this time, and I have to go over to the bathroom to grab my toothbrush.

When I turn to leave, Zahira is blocking my way out.

"Dany," she says. "What are you doing?"

"You're not going to help me anymore, right?" I say. "I'm leaving."

"I never said that."

"You were all freaked out!"

"Because you didn't tell me the truth!"

"So you would have helped me?" I say. "If you knew the cops were after me, you still would have helped me?"

She stutters over her answer, which means it's a big, fat, *NO*.

I could have ducked under her arm, but I choose to shove past her.

"Dany." She snatches my backpack, and I try to yank it back, but it pulls something in my side and my hands loosen in the sudden jolt of pain. Zahira holds my backpack far behind her and says, "I'm not letting you go out there by yourself."

"I don't need you to *let* me do *anything.*" I grab for my backpack, but she holds me away by my shoulder, gripping my hoodie so hard I'm sure it'll be misshapen for life. "Give it back!"

"Dany!" She drops my backpack, and she's lucky there isn't anything fragile inside because otherwise I would have lost it. She grabs both my shoulders, sinking down to her knees so I can see in her eyes that she's all business. "Dany. Stop it!"

I tear myself out of her grip and stagger back, and I must have finally gotten Marisa's glare down because Zahira shrinks away.

"Give it back," I say again.

"Is it true?"

"What?"

"That you were kidnapped?"

"No!"

"Then why did they say that? Why did they say that on the news?"

I don't want to answer. My side is burning and I feel the numb tingling of sparks crawling up my arms and I'm dizzy with anger, but I keep my glare as steady as I can.

"What happened at the high school?" she asks. "Were you there when it happened? Is that how you got hurt?"

"Just give me my backpack," I snap.

She clenches up her hands like she wants to hammer them down, but in the end she just releases a groan of a sigh and drops them at her sides.

"I want to help you," she says. Slowly, like it's taking everything to keep her anger at bay. "I want to get you to Ornament City. I want to make sure you're safe. But I need the truth. You don't have to tell me your entire life story. I just want to know the *truth*."

My arms are burning up to my shoulders. Up to my collarbones. All the way down my spine. But it's hard to do my breathing exercises when Zahira is staring at me like she wants to peel me apart and search my pulp for answers.

"Dany." Her voice is a lot softer now, though still simmering. "What happened at the high school?"

I can't look at her. I just stare at my backpack, trying hard to ignore the blackness creeping in the corners of my eyes.

"Did *she* do that?"

"No," I say sharply.

"Then who did?"

She waits. And somehow that's worse than the question.

I spit out, "There were people after me, okay?"

"The cops?"

"*No.*" I hate that she doesn't get it. I hate that I have to explain it. I wish she could just magically *know* and I wouldn't have to say any of it. "People. Doctors. They pretended I got kidnapped so the cops would look for me, and they got us in the high school and—and—" And my voice crumbles.

After a while, Zahira says, quietly, "What happened to Marisa?"

Oh, no. Oh, no no no. I can feel my insides crumpling, a sharp pain growing in my chest until I double over, gasping. No, Dany. Don't cry. Keep yourself together. Don't do it. Don't cry.

"Dany. Dany." Zahira grips my shoulders, holding me steady. "Dany. I'm sorry. I'm sorry. Hey. Look."

I don't want to look. My tears are hot on my cheeks, and I don't want her to see me like this. But when I lift my head, I see the sympathy in her eyes is real, and it makes me want to crumple again.

"Dany," she says. "Are they still after you?"

I swallow a sob and nod.

"What would they do if they found us?"

Us. There isn't supposed to be an *us.* I shouldn't have asked Zahira for help. I should just go right now and leave her out of it. Her and JJ and Aaron. But I need to get to Suddence, and I can't do it on my own, and I don't know what I would do if I can't get there, and—

"Dany," Zahira says firmly. "I'm not going to run away. I'm not going to leave you. But I need to know. What are they going to do?"

"They'll take me." I say, the words like acid in my chest. "And they'll kill you."

I wake up feeling like my whole body shrank into crust. I can't remember where I am or why it's so bright or why there are weird loud *whoooooooshes* coming from the sky. Car. Somewhere. Underpass? No, under an overpass.

Marisa is still sleeping. It's weird because she's always awake before me.

I turn around and say, "Marisa?" and push her shoulder. I feel so, so relieved when she makes a small groan and rolls around to face me. She looks worse than last night. She's paler and it makes the circles under her eyes look like reddish bruises. Her skin looks like wax. I don't think it's good.

"Is it morning?" she asks. Her voice sounds like sandpaper. Her eyes are still closed.

"Yes," I say, even though it doesn't feel like it. The world is all grey today. It looks like it'll rain. Or snow. I hope it won't.

Marisa tries to sit up, but she's shaking a lot. I help her lean against the side of the car. She really doesn't look okay. But before I can say it, she says. "Pass me my bag."

I do what she says. She digs out our stash of granola bars and half a bottle of water. I search my bag too and find a chocolate protein bar and a rice cracker that has probably been there for weeks because I don't remember where it came from and it's all crumbled inside the package. There's also my tube of disgusting cough syrup candy. A part of me feels guilty about buying it, which is stupid, I know. It was only a dollar. But still.

I keep the grape candy hidden and take out the protein bar and cracker. We eat our sad little breakfast, and then I ask, "What now?"

Marisa rubs her eyes. She looks like she's having a hard time keeping them open. "Drive south. Get closer to the border. Get any chance we can to cross. It's not ideal, but it's the only thing we can do."

That doesn't sound much like a plan. But I don't have a better one.

"You need medicine," I say.

Marisa climbs into the driver's seat. "I can make it."

"Make it where?"

"I'll be okay. Just give me more water."

"You need medicine."

"*I'll be okay.*"

Marisa never snaps at me. That's how I know she must be really, really sick.

I give her the water. I haven't changed my mind. Marisa needs medicine. But it's obvious bringing it up now won't get us anywhere.

I crawl into the passenger seat, and Marisa turns on the engine. The low fuel light flashes orange. She doesn't seem to notice.

"We're running out of gas," I say.

She blinks at the little gas pump icon and runs a hand across her forehead. "Okay," she says in a sigh. "Gas first."

When there's less cars around, she pulls away from the overpass and gets onto the road. It takes only ten minutes to find a gas station, but Marisa already seems a lot worse. She's squinting even though it's not very bright. Her breathing is harder than normal. And her knuckles are white on the steering wheel, like it's taking all her strength just to hang on.

When we stop at the station, she has to take a second to brace herself before she opens the door. But the moment she steps out, she suddenly covers her mouth, and then she's leaning over and puking her guts out.

"Marisa?" I say. I unbuckle and crawl to the

driver's seat. She's not puking anymore, but she's gasping real hard, and she's incredibly pale and incredibly sweaty. "Marisa?"

"I'm okay," she says. She sounds like her throat is all closed up. "I'm just a little dizzy."

I'm not sure how she expects me to believe that when I just saw her upchuck our sad little breakfast all over the concrete.

I look around. It's like 7am and we're in the countryside, so the only people here are the gas station store workers. I don't think they noticed somebody puked on their property yet, and I don't want them to because then they'd come over and ask if we need help and then they'd get a good look at our faces and snitch on us.

I help Marisa sit back in the car. She looks sick. I know I keep saying it, but that's all I can think when I see her. She's *sick,* and I don't know how long she can last like this.

"We need to find somewhere to rest," I say. "Like, *really* rest."

Marisa shakes her head, pressing her palms into her eyes. "We have to keep moving."

"We can't keep moving if you look like you're going to pass out."

"I just need to sit awhile."

"You need *medicine.*"

"We *can't get medicine,*" she bursts out, slicing

with both hands. "We can't go to a hospital. We can't go to a shelter. We have to keep going before I get worse and we are wasting time. Get in the car."

I want to cry. But I say, "You didn't pump the gas yet."

She says a bad word under her breath and starts to get out of the car. I watch her wobble, and my heart cramps with frustration.

"I'll do it," I say.

She looks like she wants to argue, but then there's some relief on her face, too. Like she's glad she doesn't have to get up.

I've never pumped gas before, but I've seen her do it enough times. I go to the gas station store and pick out some supplies first. Food and water and tissue. I pause at the little medicine section and try to figure out what Marisa needs. We have some painkiller already, but I don't know if it helps. Cold medicine? Fever medicine? Aspirin?

I hesitantly take the fever medicine and bring my haul to the counter.

The cashier has been watching me the moment I stepped in, and now she says, "You're all alone, kid?"

"No," I say. "My mom is in the car. She wants me to practice my grownup skills."

She looks at me like I'm precious.

I ask for forty liters on pump one. I pay with the cash we stole from the vending machines.

When I'm back at the car, I give Marisa the fever medicine. She slants me a look, and if she were stronger she might have given me an earful about wasting money, but now she just opens the box without a word.

I wrestle the pump into the side of the car and listen to the glug of the gas. When I glance at Marisa, she's having trouble opening the pill bottle.

I take it from her and open it easily. Fear burns like a low fire in my heart. This isn't right. Marisa shouldn't be weaker than me.

"Marisa," I start.

But she just says, "I'll be okay."

The pump clicks. I return it to its holster and get back in the car. As we pull out of the station, I glance at Marisa again, hoping to see signs that the medicine is working. Maybe she'll be less pale, or her eyes would be less dull, and there wouldn't be that tremor in her hands. I know medicine doesn't work so fast, but I can't help but feel disappointed when I see nothing has changed.

I CAN SEE the effect the word *kill* has on Zahira, and it almost makes me wish I didn't tell her that. She's frozen. Completely frozen.

And then the ice cracks and she looks like she might just melt right through the floorboards.

"Okay." She wilts back, and Aaron steadies her. She doesn't squirm away at the contact. Her eyes are unfocused, and I can tell she's turning that word over and over in her head.

Kill.

"Okay," she says again, breathlessly, and I watch her with eyes still blurry with tears. There's no fight behind what she's saying. No strength. *Okay,* not because she means it. *Okay,* because there is nothing else she can say.

Some kind of calm settles over me. This is it, then. The last time I'll see her. She won't come with me anymore.

And that's the way it should be.

While she's busy blinking away her daze and Aaron is trying to calm her down, I skirt around them and grab my backpack.

"Wait," Zahira says. She sounds like she's about to throw up. "Dany, wait, where are you going?"

"Away," I say, and march to the door.

"No," she says.

"You're scared. That's fine. I'm leaving."

"Dany, I'm taking you. I *told* you I'm taking you."

I whirl around. "Why? Did you hear *anything* I just said?"

"Yeah, I heard they're going to *take you*. You think I'm going to let that happen?"

Let. *Let.* It's always that *let*. "So, what?" I say. "You're fine with dying?"

"No," she snarls. "I'm *not* fine with dying. But I'm not fine with letting them take you, either."

"Zahira," Aaron says.

"What?"

"We should call the cops."

Zahira draws back. "What the *hell* are you talking about?"

"The TV. They said we should call the cops."

"No!"

"Maybe they can help."

"Did you not hear what Dany said? The cops are working with—with *Them*. They're not going to help us."

"So what are we supposed to do?"

"Not *we*," she says, jabbing a finger in his chest. "Just me and Dany."

Us, my own thoughts echo back at me. *There isn't supposed to be an us.* But Zahira is still brute-forcing her way into this, and I don't know how to feel. Part of me is thankful. The other part sneers, *idiot.*

"You stay here with JJ," she goes on. "Tell him whatever you think he'll believe. And for god's sake, don't do anything stupid. We're leaving now."

"Leaving?" JJ says at the kitchen door, and thank the almighty lord none of us flinch because that would *really* telegraph something is wrong. "But...what about dinner?"

"I'm sorry," Zahira says, and I'm impressed by how quickly she can school her scared face into a calm one. It reminds me of Marisa—no. No more thoughts of Marisa. "Family emergency. Something happened, and I—we have to go right now."

"It can't wait?" JJ asks. His eyes are so big and worried that it makes me feel guilty for leaving him. But I'd feel even more guilty if I stayed and got him into trouble.

Zahira says, "I'm sorry. It can't. You can put the baklava in the freezer for now. And I need to borrow your car. I'll bring it back tomorrow, I promise."

"Well." JJ looks troubled, his eyes going between me and Zahira and Aaron like he might be able to catch the secret hovering between us. "Well. Okay. The keys are on the plate in the entryway."

"Thank you." She hugs JJ, which seems to startle him. "I'm sorry. And I—I'll bring it back in time for the date. Promise."

I wish she hadn't said that. Now I have to make sure she keeps that promise.

Zahira gathers her stuff, and JJ watches, wringing his hands. As we leave, he says, "Bye! Nice to meet you!"

I clutch the edge of the door. I should turn around. I should look at him one last time. Smile. Apologize. Say a proper goodbye. It's the least I can do, after everything he's done for me.

But if I see his big, dark eyes again, I will fall apart.

"Goodbye," I say through the door, and pull it shut before I can change my mind.

"*Marisa.*"

Her head snaps up from the steering wheel. The cars behind us are honking like a whole fleet of geese.

I say, "Green light." And I point, because Marisa looks lost and confused. I'm not sure how long she can keep driving like this. We've been driving for hours on our full tank of gas, and we definitely have money for more, but that's not going to mean anything if she crashes us into a ditch.

Marisa drives forward. One of the cars behind us skirts ahead and the driver gives her the middle finger. She doesn't seem to notice, so I return the gesture for her, slamming the horn and thrusting my finger as far forward as I can.

Marisa says, "Okay, Dany, sit back."

I do as she says, even though I'm still angry. Marisa manages to drive a few blocks before her head starts dipping again. I don't know how it's possible she got paler. She reminds me of a wilting flower.

"Marisa," I say.

She doesn't answer. I guess she's struggling too much to stay awake.

It's almost dinnertime now. Dark and cold and it started to snow, just a little. We didn't take many breaks, except one at the highway rest stop where we used the washroom and ate our lunch as quickly as we could. Then we just drove and drove and drove. I'm sure we're close to the border now. Marisa still hasn't told me how she plans to cross it. Maybe we'll just ram through it with our car. Would that work? I have no idea what kind of fences the border has.

The car swerves, and I hear Marisa gasp back awake.

"Marisa," I say again.

"Dany, we've talked about this," she says. "I'm not stopping until we reach the border."

"We won't reach the border if we get in a car crash."

"We are not getting in a car crash."

"You're literally passing out on the wheel."

"No, I'm not. I'm awake. I'm—"

"Stop!"

Marisa slams the breaks. The front of the car skids way past the crosswalk line, and the person in the headlight skitters back.

For a second we just stare at him. A teenager, eyes wide, his curly hair pressed low by his beanie. He stares back, clutching the straps of his backpack, his chest heaving.

He hurries across the street and vanishes.

I didn't realize how worked up I am until now, when I go limp in my seat, sweat cold in my armpits and my head buzzing. Marisa sinks back slowly, her breaths short and quick, her fingers white around the steering wheel.

We both sit in the flashing yellow crosswalk light, staring straight ahead. The only sound comes from the windshield wipers, squelching across the glass to clear the flurry of snow.

I told you so is such an immature thing to say when we could have killed someone. But in my heart, I feel it: *I told you so. I told you so.*

Tears blur my eyes. I imagine the front of the car buckling as it hits the teenager, his body like a ragdoll as the force throws him back. He didn't look that much older than me.

Marisa keeps driving. Five minutes later, she pulls into a twisty neighbourhood lined with massive trees. She's listening to me. We're stopping for the night.

The snow comes down harder, turning to slush when it hits the windshield. We have the heater on now, but we always turn it off when we go to sleep. I'm already shivering thinking of trying to sleep in this weather. Last night was already awful. And Marisa is sick. She needs somewhere warm. Somewhere to really, properly rest.

As we wind through the neighbourhood, searching for an inconspicuous spot to park, I watch the houses passing by. They're decorated with string lights in all sorts of colours. Some even have extra ornaments out on their snowy lawns. Dainty reindeers and blown-up snowmen, jolly and round. It seems so happy and magical out there. It isn't fair.

I spy a school across a large field. The streetlamps give enough light for me to tell it's covered in construction scaffolding.

"Over there," I tell Marisa.

We park a little away from the school and walk back to it. I have to keep Marisa's arm around me so she doesn't get blown away by the wind. We round over to the school's front entrance, and I squint at the sign on the rusty construction fence.

PERMITTED HOURS OF CONSTRUCTION

Monday-Friday: 7 A.M. to 6 P.M.
Saturday: 8 A.M. to 5 P.M.
Sunday and Holidays: Prohibited

The school is under whatever an "infrastructure upgrade" is. I doubt the furnace and electricity will be working, but on the other side of the fence are a few cargo-box-shaped construction offices. THOSE would have heating, I bet.

I look at the sign again. Good. It's Friday night, and tomorrow is a stat holiday, so we have two whole days to rest up.

I'm about to spark through the chain holding the fence shut, but Marisa stops me. "In my wallet," she says, and I grumble. She's talking about her lockpicks. Leave no trace, cardinal rule number nine. Or ten? I don't remember. It's pretty far down the list.

Marisa clutches her arms close to her and shivers while I do the lockpicking. I'm not really that good at it, but eventually the lock clatters open, and I pull the fence aside enough for Marisa to fit through.

I pick the lock on the cargo box labeled "Main Office" too, and shove the door open. It looks like an office, alright. Two long skinny tables run down the middle of it, surrounded by uncomfortable-looking foldable chairs. There's a big whiteboard and a lot of clipboards and a copying machine and even a small kitchen with a coffee pot.

I help Marisa into one of the chairs and shut

the door. Even without the heating on, just being out of the wind and snow tricks me into thinking it's warm.

"I'll find some water," I say, and go over to the kitchen. I find a few bottles of water, but no food. I guess the construction guys ate it all.

I peek through the shades at the school. There's got to be food in the cafeteria.

"Here." I open a bottle of water for Marisa and make sure she drinks it. "I'm going to go inside the school to look for food. Maybe they'll have blankets and stuff, too."

Marisa lowers the bottle and wipes her lips. Her eyes are closed. She's probably dizzy. "Be careful," she says. "We need a signal, if something goes wrong."

"Nothing's going to go wrong," I say. "There's nobody here."

"Just in case." She thinks for a second. Even that seems to be a lot of work for her. "Fire alarm," she finally says. "If anything happens..."

"Got it." I spot a little radiator by the whiteboard and turn it on. I had one of these in my townhouse room. They take forever to heat up. I move it closer to Marisa. "And if something goes wrong here, shoot your gun."

That gets a weak laugh from her, but I'm serious. Why would she bother to think of a signal for me but not for herself? All our plans and cardinal rules include both of us. Just because she's a grownup doesn't mean she can't be in trouble, too.

I tell her I'll be right back, and brave the cold to get to the school. I start to pick the lock on the front door, but my fingers are too numb, so I just spark it open. Who cares, anyway? By the time the workers come back and notice, we'll already be far, far away.

I step into the lobby. The inside of the school is covered in scaffolding, too, and the floor is protected with clear tarps and cardboard duct-taped together. I spot a first aid room beside the office and rummage through its cabinets until I find a stack of orange blankets. Perfect. They feel nice and soft and warm.

Next up: food.

I wander down the main hallway until I come to a big circular cafeteria, its tables all folded up and stored near the walls. The outer edge of the circle is lined with lockers. They're almost taller than I am. I open one, expecting to see it stuffed with textbooks and binders and magazine cutouts of celebrities, but it's empty.

Focus, Dany.

Across from the food stand are two vending machines. I spark them open and fill up my backpack with energy bars, chocolate, sports drinks, and a bottle of milky coffee. It's not Marisa's favourite flavour, but it'll have to do.

I see a washroom sign jutting out by the

cafeteria and check it for running water, so we might be able to get cleaned up in the gym showers. I twist the sink handle and hold my breath as the faucet gurgles, but a tap can only cough and gasp for so long before it's clear there's no water. I shut it off more violently than I mean to.

At least I got what I came for.

I start back towards the main hallway, my backpack so heavy it hurts my shoulders. Halfway across the empty cafeteria though, I stop and turn in a circle.

This is it. The place I've seen in so many movies. This is where kids form into cliques and eat their lunches and flick mashed potato at each other. Where elaborate promposals are made and musical numbers break out and food fights are battled. I'm here, and it's empty and dark and cold, but I'm here.

I imagine sitting at a table with my friends, unpacking lunch that Marisa prepared for me. Sandwich and fruit and a cookie. That was what she packed for me every day in elementary school. Sometimes it's ham and cheese with orange and chocolate chip. Sometimes it's marmalade with apple and ginger snap. I would sit here and talk about trigonometry with my friends, complain about homework, whisper about who we think are cute.

This is the future I wanted.

It feels so...childish.

Marisa is sick. I'm cold to the bone. In two days, we'll be running again.

I still want this future. I wish it were mine. My chest aches just thinking about it.

But I can't have it.

And one day, I'll have to be okay with it.

But for now, I let myself grieve.

WE TAKE THE ELEVATOR down to the basement. I watch the floor numbers tick down, my racing heart urging it to go faster, faster, faster. It's hard not to bend around the pain in my side, or grip the elevator's railing like my life depends on it. I just press on the wound through my pocket and try to do my breathing exercises as quietly as possible. The moment Zahira notices something is wrong is the moment she takes me to the hospital instead, and I can't afford any more setbacks.

We finally reach the basement, and as we're opening the door to the garage, there's a flurry of footsteps echoing down the stairwell, and goddamn Aaron bursts from the doorway.

"Wait," he calls, out of breath. "I'm coming with you."

"No, you are not," Zahira says, shutting the garage door.

He catches it before it fully closes and hurries ahead of us. I scowl at him. I've made it this far without talking to him, but I swear, if he doesn't leave us alone—

"I can drive," he says, still a little breathless, and it's

the first time I get the sense he has a spine.

"*I* can drive," Zahira growls, trying to push past him.

"You don't know how to drive stick-shift."

"Yes, I do."

"You mean the time you drove it into that rich dude's car? That time?"

If I didn't hate Aaron so much, I might have laughed. I keep my eyes fixed on JJ's car, but out of the side of my mouth, I say to Zahira, "Do you want me to mess him up?"

"You have *cops* after you!" Aaron cries. "You have—you have people who might *kill* you! You think if they see you, you'll be able to *Fast & Furious* your way out of it?"

"Just go away," Zahira snaps, her clear voice echoing in the dim garage. We reach JJ's car, but Aaron cuts in front of us, his eyes burning with the clear message of *I'm not giving up.*

"Go. Away," Zahira seethes.

"Please, I want to help."

"Go away, or I'll let Dany mess you up."

He frowns, his mouth half open, his eyes darting to me, and I remember that he doesn't know about my power yet. I level him an icy look, crossing my arms.

"Look." He presses his hands together. "I...I messed up. I know I did. And I don't want you to think I don't know that. But you don't care that I apologized, and I want to...I just want you to know that..."

"Did you?" says Zahira.

"Did I what?"

"Apologize." She shifts her weight back, her arms crossed. "Go on. Say you're sorry."

He opens his mouth, but seems to have to wrestle the

words out. "I am."

Zahira shakes her head. "You can't even say it." She shoves him aside and unlocks the car door. I round to the passenger side. I need to sit down before my side finally decides to explode.

"No, wait," Aaron blurts, and I groan. "I'm sorry. I really am. I'm sorry."

Zahira holds his gaze for a good long while. Then, slowly, she nods, like she's still mad but knows Aaron really means it. "Good."

She gets in the car and pulls on her seatbelt.

"Zahira, please," he says. "Let me help."

Zahira ignores him and tries to start the engine.

"Clutch," Aaron says.

"I knew that," Zahira grinds through her teeth, and peers beneath the dashboard to locate it. Eventually she manages to put the car in reverse, but when she starts to back out of the parking spot, the car lurches with a puttering sound, and I cling to the seatbelt as she cusses.

"You're releasing the clutch too fast," Aaron points out. At least he's not condescending about it.

Zahira tests the clutch, inching the car back a little more, but when the engine stalls again, she stops, gripping the wheel hard with annoyance. Aaron puts his hands on his hips and lowers his head, sighing.

"Come on," he pleads.

"Aaron," Zahira says. "Understand something. This isn't me trying to make you feel bad. I can't let you drive us."

"Why?"

"Because it's dangerous."

He opens his arms, his eyes wide. "And I can help you *out* of that danger!"

Zahira sags back with a gnash of her teeth, but when she looks at me, the message is clear. I tip my head and groan.

"Only if you're okay with it," she says, as if there's much of a choice.

"Fine," I say. Not because I like Aaron all of a sudden, but because the pain in my side is getting serious now, and I can't bear another second sitting here idle while it gets worse.

Zahira cusses under her breath and shoves open the door. "Alright," she says crankily. "Get in."

With a shower of *thank you's,* Aaron slips into the driver's seat. Zahira kicks me out of the passenger seat, and I'm stuck in the back with the trash again.

"Just so we're clear," Zahira says, "this doesn't make us friends. It just means that when I speak to you, I'll be a little less pissed."

Aaron nods vigorously.

And then finally, *finally,* we're pulling out of the garage and seeking a path to the highway. Zahira pulls out our book of maps and begins recalculating our route.

"Where am I driving to?" Aaron asks.

"Ornament City," says Zahira. "Downtown."

"That's *far.*"

"You wanted to come," she snaps. "What did you tell JJ, anyway?"

"The truth," Aaron says, shrugging. "That you suck at stick-shift."

Zahira slaps his shoulder with the atlas, and here I

am, stuck being the third wheel again.

"Anywhere in downtown?" Aaron asks, glancing at me. "Or like, a specific street?"

Anywhere, I'm about to say, but when my side protests, I bite the word back. I could barely walk forty minutes down the highway. I can barely stand the pain now, even through the medicine. How long is the walk up the winding road leading into Suddence? An hour? Two?

I don't want Aaron and Zahira to come with me. No one is supposed to know where I'm going. *Leave no trace,* Marisa says. But this is the only way I'll get there.

I say, "I'm not going to Ornament City."

Zahira gives me a look that could slice me in half. "Where, then?"

She's angry that I lied to her, I can tell. But I don't have the will to snap back with my excuses, so I just say, "I'm going to Suddence."

"Suddence," Aaron says. "Where's that?"

I find it in the atlas for them. It's actually a little closer than Ornament City, which seems to give Zahira some relief. Aaron does the math, and estimates we should arrive by 1 A.M.

Zahira sits back with a sigh and cuts me another look. "Alright. Come on. Spill it." Then she adds, "*All* of it."

I sink into the seat. Like the road to Suddence, *all of it* is long and winding and painful, but I tell it.

I tell them about Johnny McKay and the clinic and Doctor Heed and Lilian.

I tell them about our two years on the run and The Stadium Incident and The Motel Incident.

I tell them about Marisa, how she took care of me all

this time, how she suddenly became sick.

But I stop when I get to the high school, my throat sore from talking and the reminder of what happened next.

Going by Zahira's expression, she doesn't expect me to tell this part, anyway.

"That's it," I say, perfectly aware of how tight my voice is. I keep my eyes fixed out the windshield, hoping the familiar sight of the road would lift the weight on my chest. "Happy?"

"That's not exactly the word I'd use," Zahira mutters.

To his credit, Aaron has been quiet through the whole story, but now he says, "Sparks?"

To prove it, I stick my hand between the front seats and call up a cluster of pinprick stars dancing over my palm.

"Oh," he says weakly.

Yeah. *Oh*.

I sit back, releasing a long breath. The story leaves me exhausted, and so does the pain, but I don't try to sleep. If we get spotted by cops and they give us a chase, I have to be ready. I can't let my guard down. I'm too close to have it all be ruined by carelessness.

The first hour passes without incident.

So does the second.

By the third, Zahira is yawning, and so am I, but I keep my eyes open.

We're almost there.

We're almost there.

I bring everything back to Marisa. She's looking a little better. No, that's not right. She still looks like all the colour bled out of her. But at least she looks calmer. She sits straighter when she sees me come in.

"All good," I say. I spread the blankets on the ground, forming one into a pillow, and help Marisa sit in the makeshift bed. I drape the last blanket over her knees. The heater is doing a great job warming up the room, but Marisa is still shivering.

"Here." I give her the energy drink and some granola bars. I put my jacket over the nearest chair, and when I turn back, Marisa is having trouble ripping open the granola bar package, like she's too weak to even grip her fingers together, so I go over and do it for her.

Instead of *thank you,* she says, "I'm sorry."

"Why?" I say.

"I don't know." Her hand droops, and for a second I'm afraid she's about to drop the granola bar, but she just buries her eyes in her other hand. And she's crying. She's *crying.* I don't like seeing her like this.

"Don't cry." That's such a stupid, useless thing to say. I don't know what I'm supposed to do though. I've never had to comfort anyone before. I want to beg her to stop crying. I want to tell her she's scaring me. But I know it's not going to help. I reach forward and hug her instead.

It takes her a few long, long seconds to hug me back, and I can't remember the last time we hugged. When I started elementary school, I always dodged out of her hugs because I didn't want her to treat me like a baby who needed to be coddled. I was going to school. I was growing up. But right now, I don't feel so grown-up. I feel so small, and I need her. I need her.

"Dany." I can still hear tears in her voice. She pulls away and looks me dead in the eyes, her hands tight on my shoulders. "Listen to me. This is serious. If tomorrow I am too weak to move, you need to go on without me. You hear? Take what you can and go."

"I don't know how," I say. "Not on my own."

"Yes, you do. We've talked about this."

I shake my head desperately. We've talked about getting separated. We've never talked about me leaving her *forever.*

She grips me tighter. I can tell it's taking all her strength because her hands are shaking. "We're close to the border now. Just a day's walk. You can't cross without a passport, so you *find—*" She stops to catch her breath. "You get away from where all the people are. You find a part of the fence that has no guards. In the prairies. Or in the woods. There will be cameras, so you need to be fast. Spark through, and *run.* Just *run.*"

I can't. The words are about to burst out, burning my throat raw. *I can't.*

"Dany." She moves one hand to the side of my head, smoothing down my hair. She still looks like a picture that is fading away, but her eyes are burning with determination. "You can do it. I know you can."

I imagine myself at the border's chain-link fence. I imagine sparking a hole in it. I imagine running, running, running.

Alone.

"And then what?" I say.

Her face crumples, and quietly, she says, "I don't know."

"I don't want to leave you," I say, and nothing else because I know my voice is about to break.

"I know, baby. I know." She folds around me, and I bury my face in her coat, and I want to cry, but one of us has to stay strong.

I don't know how long we hold each other until she speaks again. "Dany," she says in that thin broken voice. "I need to tell you something. It's a last resort. Promise me, you'll only use it as a last resort."

I don't have a clue what she might be talking about, but I nod, my face still buried.

"I need to write it down. I need paper."

I don't want to let go of her, but I wipe my eyes and search the office. I come back with a marker and a pad of sticky notes, and Marisa begins writing on it with trembling hands.

Numbers. A phone number.

She folds the note up and presses it into my hand. "Last resort," she says. "Promise?"

"Who is it?"

"Promise."

I swallow and say, "I promise."

There's no relief in her eyes when I say this, but I see acceptance, like she's done all she can do, and I want to tell her, *No! This isn't all you can do! You have to come with me! You can't leave me alone!*

The words stay burning in my throat. I pour myself into her arms again. I want to lie down and sleep and hope when tomorrow comes, it'll be a fresh start. The snow will cover the grey of the world, and Marisa will be okay.

I make sure she eats and drinks and takes some medicine. I eat, too, and try to imagine leaving the school tomorrow morning, on my own, without Marisa. But my mind won't bend that way.

I can't leave her.

The thought is a wall in my head, red-brick and strong.

I can't leave her.

I can't leave her. And I can't survive without her. It's not my sparks keeping me alive. It's *her.* And I don't know what I'd do without her.

I don't want to be alone.

We sleep back-to-back again, with the orange blankets and radiator keeping us warm. The sickness puts Marisa in a deep sleep, but I stay wide awake, waiting. Waiting until it's way past midnight, and the world is asleep.

Dear diary. I forgot about you for a hot second, huh?

I have to tell you a secret.

I'm not going to leave Marisa.

I'm going to save her.

WAY AFTER MIDNIGHT, we reach the road to Suddence.

It's so unimpressive that we drove right past it before rounding back. Aaron said he thought it was a maintenance side road. I can't blame him. It really does look like one, the gate low and old and covered in rust and some kind of moss. It doesn't help that the yellow sign on it says *Authorized Access Only*.

"You sure this is it?" Aaron asks, like he's hoping we'll say no.

Zahira consults the map. "That's what it says."

I stare up the road. We've been rumbling down a country road for the last thirty minutes. It's so rural that there aren't any streetlamps, and the big evergreen trees and the cracked asphalt only made the journey even creepier.

The road leading up to Suddence doesn't ease up on the creep. It's much narrower than the country road, and grass is growing through the pavement, and the trees are bending over it like they want to swallow it alive.

Zahira turns to me. "You're sure Suddence is up

there?"

I don't know. It has to be.

I nod.

"Okay, then," Aaron says, and swings the car up towards the gate. I spark the lock and push it open. The car tires grind through the gravel as we begin our climb.

I keep my eyes fixed on the road ahead, lit by our headlights. We go uphill, then downhill, then uphill again, twisting up a mountain path, twining back down. The car rocks over the uneven road, and I clutch the front seats for balance as I lean forward.

Eventually, the trees start to sparse out, replaced by a prairie of long grass. The moon is out from behind the winter clouds, and the field sparkles with rainwater.

"What's that?" I say.

Aaron slows the car. On the side of the road is a sign.

It's flat on the ground, half-covered in weeds and grass, rusty and old like the gate. Still, I release a breath. We're on the right track after all.

I can feel relief from Zahira and Aaron, too, but by the time I turn to look at them, worry is back on Zahira's face.

"Why is it just on the ground like that?" she says.

"Maybe they don't have the time to fix it," Aaron says

uncertainly.

They glance at me like I might have answers, but I don't.

We drive on.

It doesn't take long to reach another gate, this one huge and bright red with two doors, both with big white signs fixed to them. Aaron slows to a stop on the gravelly road. The words are too small for me to read, but the images are perfectly clear.

Red circle with a white bar. Do not enter.

Yellow triangle with a bold black exclamation mark. Caution.

The third one, though.

The third one is a dark human shape with a star erupting from its chest.

"What does that say?" Zahira says, squinting. She taps Aaron with the back of her hand. "Get closer."

The car ekes forward like Aaron is afraid of accidentally hitting a landmine. I look out the side window. The wiry fence stretches on and on, bending into the distance.

"Dany?" Zahira sounds far away, and I have to pull my mind back into the car. "Are you sure they're here?"

They're both looking at me with concern in their eyes. I know what they were expecting. A town, alive. Asleep at this time but still *alive*. We haven't even seen the town yet, but already everything is wrong. The old gates. The untended roads. The warning signs.

Something terrible happened.

I nod. I think I nod. I wasn't expecting all of this, either, but it changes nothing.

I pick up my backpack and reach for the door.

"*No,*" Zahira and Aaron blurt at the same time. They glance at each other, like they're appalled to be thinking the same thing. Zahira says, "Stay in the car. It's safer. We'll drive in and let you off when we see them."

"I'll be fine," I say. "I'll just walk. It's not that far."

Zahira scowls. "Did you not read the sign?"

Nervously, Aaron mutters, "It says trespassers will be arrested."

"You're worried about trespassing?" I say flatly.

"No, he's right," says Zahira, and I can't help but notice this is the second time she's agreeing with him. "If the security guards show up, you can't outrun them."

"And you think we can out-drive them?"

"We'd have a better chance," Aaron says defensively, and I want to shoot back with *I didn't ask for your opinion.* I guess my death stare gets enough of it across though because he draws back a little, scowling.

Zahira points at the sign, at the erupting star. "You know that that means? *Health hazard.* There's something dangerous here, and whatever it is, we'll be safer in the car instead of running around unprotected."

I can tell there's more to it. She's afraid nobody is here to pick me up, and she doesn't want to leave me here, all alone in the middle of nowhere in the dead of night.

But I really, really, really don't care. I don't need her or Aaron anymore. The town is *right there.* I just need to get out of the car, and Zahira and Aaron can go away and watch musicals with JJ all day.

But I also know if I jump out of the car, they'd just barge in right after me, anyway.

"Fine." I cross my arms and lean back. With a glare, the lock on the gate snaps off.

Aaron drives forward, pushing through to the gravel road on the other side. The ground slopes upwards, and the car rocks and bumps over the lumpy hill.

Almost there. I clutch the key through my hoodie. *Almost there.*

We reach the top of the hill, and a chill pours over my skin.

In the moonlit distance, I can see the town. But my eyes only snag on it for a second before dropping down to the massive maw of a hole between us.

It's so big that my brain almost can't comprehend it. I've never seen a hole so wide or so deep. I'm not even sure I can call it a hole. It's a crater, a black hole, ringed on the sides, spiralling way, way, way down.

The car is silent, and I can tell Zahira and Aaron are trying to wrap their heads around it, too.

"It's a mine," Aaron says. Quiet, like he doesn't want to wake the beast.

"Huh?" Zahira says weakly.

"Mine," Aaron says again. "Rock mine. I never knew they were so..."

Big is the word he's looking for, but *big* seems like the wrong word for it, too. I think if I fell down the side, I would never stop falling. I try to see what's at the bottom, like that might comfort me, but my head hits the top of the car before I can see halfway down. I shiver. The deepness is so dizzying it makes me a little queasy.

"I've never heard about this," Zahira says, trying to get a good look down the mine, too. "What do you think they were mining?"

"I don't know," says Aaron.

I don't know, either. All I know is that we should stay far, far away from it.

We drive towards the town. We're a good distance away from the side of the mine, but I can't help shuddering as I imagine the ground slipping away, spilling all of us into the abyss. Some kind of panicked laugh bubbles up my throat, but I swallow it. It would be really funny if I came all this way just to fall down a pit a minute away from Suddence. Funny in a way that makes me want to shrivel up into a pulp.

I blink hard and put my focus on the town. It grows closer at the rate of a glacier. I lean forward, clutching the front seats, anticipation making my heart lurch and sputter.

This is it.

I'm here.

A wooden sign says in a flowery white font, *Welcome to Suddence!* The painting around the words shows the scenery, the prairie and the mine, all chipping and flaking away. There's no explanation of what the purpose of the mine is. No explanation for what they were looking for.

Maybe I'll never find out.

We pass the sign, and we're in the town.

The town square comes first, and I watch the buildings as we creep through. I search for signs of what might have happened here, but everything looks normal. Too normal. A grocery store. A flower shop. A clinic. A dentist. A barber. All dark, all empty, brick buildings overgrowing with vines and moss and grass. I keep expecting to see people in the windows, but there's just us and our car in the dusty reflections.

"Dany," Zahira says, hushed as she takes in the ghost town. "Are you sure somebody's here?"

"Yes," I say, my eyes still on the passing buildings.

"I don't see anyone—"

"They're here."

She goes quiet.

The shop street ends in a small courtyard. On the other side, I see the start of a neighbourhood, small houses and their little yards. My fingers find the key through my clothes again. I've studied it enough times to memorize the number on it, but I rub my thumb over the key cover like the number might have changed.

#109.

I watch the houses as we wind through the neighbourhood. It feels like a real neighbourhood, a *normal* neighbourhood, with street names and sidewalks and cul-de-sacs, and I find myself trying to see people in the windows again. Some houses still have cars parked in the driveway. One yard has a trampoline. One has plastic toddler toys sinking into the wild lawn.

I glance at the house numbers.

#9.

#11.

#13.

It might be a while before we reach #109. But that means nothing if I can't come up with a reason for Zahira and Aaron to let me out of the car by myself. I just *know* they'd rather stay here with me and wait, and I don't know what I would do if I can't convince them to go away.

We're almost past #51 when Aaron says, "Is that—?"

My head snaps forward. In the distance, at the top of the hill where we came from, is a prickle of light. A car, speeding our way.

Zahira sits straighter and glances at me. "Is that them?"

Another pair of headlights round over the hill. My pulse skitters.

"It's not them," I say. "We have to go. Let's go."

"What?" Aaron says. "How do you know?"

"It's not them!" I shout.

Zahira's eyes are wide. "Is it…is it…?"

I know she means Them, but it isn't. They can't possibly know I'm here. I yell, "Just drive!"

Aaron punches it. He manages a U-turn, heading back the way we came. We get to the little courtyard the same time the first car appears at the far end of the town, where the square begins. A truck, with yellow lights flashing on the roof.

And then there's a voice, amplified through a megaphone: "Stop the car! Turn off the engine and step out with your hands up! You are trespassing!"

"Security guards," Aaron says. *"Shit!"*

He yanks the car to the side, lurching over the curb, and aims for an alley that leads out into the field.

"Aaron!" Zahira cries, pointing. "Trash bin! Trash bin!"

"I know!" he roars, but doesn't slow down.

I cling to my seatbelt and cram my eyes shut as the car shoots between the trash bin and the alley wall. I hear something screech, and the *thunk!* of something hitting the side of the car, but when I open my eyes, the car is still in one piece, and we're racing through the field.

"Oh, god," Zahira says, and I look over to see the mirror on her side is gone, lost somewhere in the alley.

I turn in my seat, watching the town draw away through the back window. Somewhere out there, house #109 is getting farther away, and my heart aches at the thought, but panic is quick to fill me up again when Aaron cusses, and I turn back to see the second security vehicle skirting around the outside of the town square, sirens wailing, coming right towards us.

Aaron veers left, taking us farther into the field. The grass is so long we can barely see what's ahead of us.

"Go back to the gate!" Zahira shouts. "We have to get out of here!"

The grass whips past the windows. I look out the back window again and can't help cursing when I see we're leaving a path of trampled grass behind us. The security vehicle is having no trouble tracing us, their glaring headlights menacing in the night.

"Stop the car!" The voice sounds frantic. "Stop!"

The grasses suddenly vanish. Zahira screams, and Aaron slams on the brakes.

The mine looms before us, wide and unending. The car skids in the gravel, still terribly fast.

We're going to fall in.

We're going to die.

Gritting my teeth, I throw out my hands. Sparks crack against the front of the car, and the force punches us back.

The car rocks to a violent stop, the engine hood bent and buckled. A sprinkle of rocks scatter over the side of the mine.

I clutch the seatbelt burning across my chest, my head spinning. Aaron and Zahira groan and gasp, pushing at the airbags that erupted in the crash. Zahira has a bloody nose. Aaron is holding his eye.

"Step out of the car!" the security guard shouts, his voice and the sirens growing closer. "Step out of the vehicle with your hands on your head!"

Our engine is silent, dead from the shock of the sparks. Aaron twists the key, trying to reignite it, but it only sputters and sputters. The inside of our car grows brighter as the security vehicle closes in, its sirens so deafening my hands fly over my ears.

"Aaron," Zahira pleads.

"I'm trying!" he says.

I look out the back window again. The security vehicle is almost here. Our engine still isn't starting.

We're going to get caught.

No, a voice in my head snarls. *No, you're not.*

Not when you're so close.

I grab my backpack and slam open the door.

"Dany!" Zahira cries. "Dany, wait!"

I bolt. I don't care how much Zahira is screaming behind me, or how much my side shrieks along. I just press a hand to my wound and *run*, and when I hear the security vehicle change its direction towards me, I throw a blind volley of sparks towards its wheels and hear the sharp pop of rubber, the horrible scrape of the car grinding to a stop.

Just run, Dany. Just run.

I push my way back into the grass, back in the direction of the town. My feet stumble over the uneven ground. Something warm blooms on my side, over my hand. I'm tearing open my wound.

Go, Dany. You're almost there.

House #109. I just have to get there, and I just have to have enough time, and I don't care if the guards catch me afterwards—

My foot catches over a sharp drop in the dirt, and pain spears through my ankle, all the way up to my brain. I fall, crying out, and try to clamber back up, but putting weight on my twisted ankle makes me crumple again. The pain in my side isn't just warm anymore. It's a horrible heat, white-hot and blinding, and every time I try to push onto my knees, my eyes blur with boiling tears and my throat aches with wrenching sobs.

Come on, Dany. Get up. You're almost there. You're almost there.

I don't hear the guard coming until he's right beside me. "Found the runner," he says into his walkie-talkie, out of breath, and then he gasps, cussing to himself. "It's a kid. Oh my god, it's a kid."

And then he's talking to me, asking if I'm okay, if I need help. I try to push him aside, but he ends up holding me so I don't fall over. His eyes go down to my waist, to my bloody hand, and his cusses again. He pinches the side of his walkie-talkie and says, "Call an ambulance. We have an injury."

No, I want to say, but when I open my mouth, all I can do is sob. *No. Don't take me away.*

But the guard is gathering me into his arms and bringing me back to the clearing, and I'm shivering too much from the pain to fight him. *Dany!* somebody calls, through all the cotton in my ears, and I manage to look over.

Zahira. Aaron. They're out of the car, hands behind their heads. Aaron's eye is swollen shut. Zahira's pink jacket is smattered with blood. They look at me with eyes round with fear, burning with the need to run over and see what happened to me, but the other security guards have arrived, and they're flicking out their handcuffs.

No, I try to say again, and I reach out for them. My hand is filthy, smudged with dirt, scratched from the fall. Aaron. Zahira. I watch the cuffs snap over their wrists. *Stop. It's not their fault. It's mine. It's mine.*

But I'm faint from the pain, and I can't keep my hand outstretched, and slowly, slowly, the world bleeds away.

PART IV:
Last Resort

QUIETLY, I SLIP out of the cargo-box office and sneak back into the school. I already made up my mind. I'm not leaving Marisa. I just have to figure out a way to save her.

She needs medicine. And it must be something expensive, or something hard to get, or otherwise we would have gotten some from the pharmacy already. I would need to get into a hospital, and...and...

Well. I'm not sure what I'd need to do. But I know I'd need to be strong.

And maybe I'd need some help.

I find the gym, dark but orangey from the snowy sky. I sit under the basketball board and unfold the note Marisa gave me.

Last resort, she said.

Well, this is a last resort.

I slip out Marisa's cellphone. I feel bad for stealing it, but I don't have my own cellphone, and I doubt the phones in the school's office still work. I flick it open and stare at the little screen, my thumb hovering over the glow-in-the-dark numbers. Who would pick up on the other side? Social workers? Marisa's distant relatives? Whoever might be waiting for us outside the country?

Before I lose my courage, I punch in the numbers.

It rings. And rings. And rings.

When it finally picks up, my heart is racing at a zillion miles per hour.

"Marisa?" the voice on the other end says, and my pulse grinds to a stop.

Lilian.

I slam the phone shut. Lilian. Marisa said she betrayed us to the cops at the motel. Marisa said she lied.

But she's supposed to be my last resort?

The phone rings, and I can tell it's from Lilian. I decline it and shove the phone back in my pocket.

No. I'm not taking help from Lilian. She pretended to be Marisa's friend and then *tricked* her. She and her dad want to cut me apart and steal my power.

I just sit there, trying to calm myself down from the close call. Good thing I didn't say anything. Good thing I hung up before she could track us.

But now it means I'm on my own.

I stare at the other end of the gym, kneading my hands together until I'm sure they're not shaking anymore.

On my own? Fine.

I don't need anybody's help, anyway.

I haul myself to my feet. Even in the dark, I can make out the basketball lines and volleyball lines.

I remember the day at the motel. The sparks, the brightness, the heat.

If I could call them again, I would be unstoppable. I could march right into the hospital and demand the medicine and if they call the cops, I'll blast right through them.

Yeah, the cardinal rules. I know.

But this is a last resort.

I start small. A warm-up. Tiny, after-image sparks right above my palms. I can feel the slight ripples in the air, barely a tickle.

I will them farther from my hands, first upwards until they're a full head above me, and then forwards until they reach the free throw line. I make them grow, like feeding gasoline to a fire. They're the size of thumbtacks, then my hands, then the tires on a truck. The edges of the deep-purple sparks shimmer like light around a closed door, thin and fragile.

I drop my hands, catching my breath. I've never gotten my sparks to be visible on purpose before. I didn't even know it was possible until

the motel. I didn't know my sparks could be so
bright. I didn't know my sparks were like fire.

I take a deep breath and focus on the spot
above the free throw line. This time, I don't care
about the size of my sparks. I care about making
them *seen.*

I call up a spark. Again, it's only barely
visible at the edges.

Come on, Dany. Try harder.

I focus it over my palms instead. The closer,
the easier. But it's still doing that *thing*. That
flickering edges, blink-and-you-miss-it thing.

What was I feeling when I called the bright
sparks for the first time? I was hiding in the
washroom, terrified. And then I was in the
parking lot, anger boiling over.

Volatile, Marisa told me. I know calling my
sparks like this is dangerous. But I have to start
somewhere.

Angry. Afraid. I imagine the cops
surrounding the school, guns ready, about to
burst in. They're going to take you, Dany. Are
you going to just let them?

I try again. The spark is only a little brighter.

Dany, they're grabbing you, throwing you
into the car, bringing you to the police station.
They—*They!!*—are going to march right in and
take you. They are going to cut you apart.

I try again. It flickers like a candle about to
die.

They're going to cut you apart.

And They're going to kill Marisa.

Fear tunnels into my heart, cold and hollow, but I clamp hard against it. No. I won't be afraid. Afraid makes me useless. It makes me that helpless mess in the bathroom, sparks skittering out of my control, *hiding.*

I twist the fear around, wrangling it until it feels like flames in my chest. I hold my palms facing each other and concentrate, remembering the way the sparks felt between them, the wild energy trying to break through the cage.

Standing in the parking lot, fire running up my arms, down my spine. I remember I could still feel the first blast in my hands, a buzz singing through my bones, and when my anger spilled over, the second wave of bright sparks came easy, like the paths were already cleared for them.

And the thing that made my anger spill. The thing I heard, over the crackly walkie-talkie.

We have Marisa Lane coming down the road.

And all I could think was, *No.*

I can't let them take Marisa.

So I didn't.

Now, Dany. Now you have to be strong like that again. Because if you're not, Marisa will die, and it will be your fault. It will be *your fault.*

You can't let that happen.

The first bright spark bursts. There, and then gone again, leaving a real after-image in the middle of my sight. A strange, jagged firework.

A buzzing begins in my ears.

Again.

The second one comes easier. I call a third one a little ahead of me, and a fourth near the free throw line.

My head spins. I feel hot pressure on my temples.

Again.

Over the free throw line. Over the midcourt line. A little to the left. A little to the right.

Bigger.

Red-hot metal pools in my head. I try to shake the feeling away, but it only makes my head spin. I focus on the spot over the midcourt line and will my sparks to *grow.* Bright spots flicker like a string of firecrackers, each spark the size of my fist, but I need more.

They grow. Bigger by each flash, overlapping, bleeding into each other. They're so bright I can barely keep my eyes on them, and I feel the heat, waves and waves of it, and then—

And then something *snaps,* and the room lights up like a bolt of lightning. I stumble back, startled. Heat flashes against my skin, and the *sound*...not really a thunder, but like the beginning of one. A deep, dark, chest-fuzzying rumble.

I laugh. More from surprise than anything else.

And then I get so dizzy I have to sit down before I faint. My head hurts, and I'm out of breath, and I feel like I can sleep for a billion years, but I did it. My sparks. Bright and hot and terrifying and *powerful.*

I dig out one of the sports drinks I stole from the vending machine and take a long, long drink. I need to practice more. I need to be able to call the bright sparks without taking so long to psych myself up.

But first, I need to catch my breath and wait for my head to stop spinning.

I sit with my back against the wall, my legs stretched out in front of me. The ringing in my ears is slowly draining away. My arms are still tingling with the power. I watch the shadow of snow falling through the gym's windows, and I laugh again, just a small one. I can really do this. I can save Marisa.

But the little joy disappears when, somewhere down the hall, a door bangs open.

I scramble to stand up, but stop on my knees because my sight is clouding over with black. I scrabble for the wall, using it to pull myself up.

Footsteps. Far, but getting closer.

For a short, hopeful moment, I think it's Marisa. She woke up and realized I'm gone, and now she's here to look for me.

But then I hear a deep voice, *two* deep voices, and I know it isn't her at all.

IT TAKES EVERYTHING to pull my mind out of the darkness. It keeps slipping back, but I hold tight. Fingers digging into it. Dragging it forward. Dragging it up, out of the mud.

Breaking the surface feels slow. Not a gasp of air, but treading water, still sinking, still fighting.

A shard of a thought carves through the sludge. "Where's..." My lips press together, starting to form the wrong name, and it jolts me out of the mud a little more. "Where's...where's..."

I try to sit up, but a hand presses over my shoulder.

"Hey, it's okay," says a voice I don't recognize.

I force my eyes to open.

Sirens.

Ambulance.

EMT.

I blink at the rest of the car, my eyelids too heavy to stay open. One other EMT. Nobody else.

Where's...where's...

Zahira.

I lurch up, and something pinches across my chest. A strap. There's one over my thighs, too, and my hoodie is unzipped and my shirt is lifted to make room for a bulk of fresh bandages. My mind screams from the pain of moving, and suddenly I'm wide awake.

"Where is she?" I demand. "Where is she?"

"Don't worry, don't worry," EMT #1 says, putting a hand out to calm me down. "She's not here anymore. You're safe."

I struggle against the straps. I call for my sparks, but I feel weak. Empty. I sink back down, closing my eyes like that might stop the pain or make me feel better or do *anything*.

"I know you're scared," EMT #1 is saying, through the buzzing in my ears, "but you're safe now. We're on the way to the hospital. You're going to be okay."

My eyes are suddenly hot with tears. I try to blink them back, but it's impossible. I was almost there. I almost made it. And now everything's all wrong, and I don't know how far I am from Suddence, and I don't know where they took Zahira and Aaron. I can still hear Zahira's scream in my ears. *Dany, wait!*

But I left them. I betrayed them. And now they're paying for it.

"Kid," EMT #1 says carefully. "I'm going to ask you some questions, okay? This will help when we get to the hospital. The doctors there will know how to take care of you. Is that alright?"

I release a shaky breath and stare straight at the double doors.

"Here's an easy one," he says. "Can you tell me your

name?"

I glance at EMT #2. She's busy checking the machines, but she flashes me a reassuring smile when she sees me looking.

I take a deep breath to calm my tears and say, "Dany."

EMT #1 seems surprised, and I don't understand why. "Okay," he says. "Dany. Can you tell me how much pain you're in, on a scale of one to ten?"

"Two," I lie.

"And can you tell me how you got hurt?"

I stare stubbornly ahead. I don't know what it was. A shard of wood. Or glass. Or light. It came and went, and the pain was sharp, and that's all I know.

EMT #1 presses his lips together. "Okay. Um. How long ago was it when you got hurt?"

There's a deep heaviness behind my eyes, and my lungs are aching to cry, but I clench my fists and bite it all back. "A few days." I feel tears coming again and manage to blink hard against them. "Where are they? The woman and the man who were with me?"

"You don't have to worry about them anymore," EMT #1 soothes. "They're gone now. You're safe."

"No. I need to know." I hold his eyes. He has to see that I mean it. "Please. I just...I need to know."

He sighs and leans back, sadness or pity or something just as useless in his eyes. "I'm sorry, kid. I don't know."

I lie back, squeezing my eyes shut. I want to scream my frustration. I want to smash out the double doors and track Zahira and Aaron down myself. But I know I'm not strong enough for that. Not yet.

I remember the surprise on EMT #1's face when I told him my name. Only now am I piecing together why.

He knows who I am. He knows I'm the kid everyone is looking for. He knows my name, my *old* name from the posters. The name he expected me to say.

And he must have called it in. He must have reported it to the hospital, or worse, the cops.

And that means They know where I am now.

My mind is racing, but there's nothing I can do. Nothing except lie here and grit my teeth and wait for my sparks to come back.

I don't know how I'm going to find Aaron and Zahira.

But I know I have to find them before They do.

I GRAB MY backpack and run. Or at least, I try to, but the ground teeters and the world turns into a long tunnel, and my knees bang hard on the ground.

Luckily for me, the two deep voices don't seem to hear me. I scramble back, pressing against the wall, and pray pray *pray* they won't come into the gym.

Their footsteps clip by the gym doors. A flashlight clicks on, and in the faint light, I can tell it's two cops.

"...can't believe we have to be here in the middle of the night," Cop #1 grumbles.

"It's probably just those kids smoking weed again, anyway," Cop #2 says. The flashlight beam swings around. "Hey, come on out, you little punks!" he shouts, as if anyone would be dumb enough to answer.

They're almost past the gym now. I brace my

feet on the ground. The moment they're gone, I'm making a dash for the door, and I hope the duct tape around my left shoe will hold.

But they stop walking. "What's that smell?" Cop #2 says.

Cop #1 sniffs. "Firecrackers?"

And they come towards the gym's side doors.

I haul myself to my feet, but I'm too late. The doors open, and the flashlight beam finds me.

"Hey!" Cop #1 shouts.

I bolt. I slam the gym doors open, sprinting full speed for the front doors, but my dizziness catches up to me, and I stumble. Cop #2 snatches my arm and spins me around. He has me by both shoulders, and anger is boiling in his eyes, but then his expression goes slack.

"Oh my god," he says. "You're—"

I stomp him in the shin. He hollers. I tear myself out of his grip and fall back against one of the lobby columns. I need to run. I need to warn Marisa. But my vision is turning black again, and I can't catch my breath, and by the time I notice Cop #1 has caught up, he's already reaching out to grab me.

I spin away, losing my balance for a second, but I push off the ground and race back into the gym.

Come on, sparks, I plead, reaching for the fire, the unbearable buzz up my arms, but it's like I'm scraping the bottom of a well. *Come on!*

"Call it in!" Cop #1 shouts behind me. "I'll chase!"

Oh, no. Don't call it in. I turn, thinking to spark Cop #2's walkie-talkie, but Cop #1 is catching up way too fast. I shove through the side doors, my lungs burning, and bolt down the hallway, the darkness cut through by Cop #1's flashlight.

I need somewhere to hide. Somewhere to calm down and rest and wait for my sparks to recover.

And—and *Marisa.* I have to warn her.

I skid out into the cafeteria. My eyes land on a bright red box on the wall.

Fire alarm. Our signal.

I dive for it. The white handle snaps down.

Nothing happens.

I keep running, waiting for the deafening wail to come on. Maybe the system is just old. Maybe the system is just slow.

Or maybe the system was disconnected for the construction.

Across the cafeteria, I spy another alarm and pull it.

Still nothing.

"Hey!" Cop #1 shouts, huffing and puffing. "Kid, stop running!"

He's slowing down from exhaustion, but so am I. I clutch the lockers for balance and call for my sparks again. The moment I feel a glimmer of something, I hurl it at Cop #1, but I might as well have thrown a speck of dust at him for how much he's unfazed.

He slows to a walk, his hands on his knees as he catches his breath. This is my chance to shove him over and keep running, but I'm out of breath, my skull squeezing around my brain and my legs turning to jelly.

"Kid," Cop #1 gasps, wiping his forehead. "I'm...not going...to hurt you. I want to help, okay?"

I back away. I don't care if he sounds like he means it. He has no idea what me and Marisa are up against.

My back hits a door handle. I twist it and, quick as quicksilver, I dodge into the room and shove a chair against the handle.

The door rattles. Cop #1 is trying to get in.

"Kid," he says again. "I promise. You're safe now. You don't have to be afraid anymore."

I huddle against the wall and close my eyes. I hold my hands up, palms facing each other, and try to imagine sparks coming between them again, the feeling of a storm desperate to break free. But the little sliver I feel is too far away, and my shaking arms are too weak to pull it in.

Come on, Dany. Think fast. Cop #2 is already calling it in. If you don't do something, They're going to march right in.

So *do something.*

"I know this is scary," Cop #1 says. "I know

we seem scary. But we're here to help you, okay? Where's your mom? Is she here with you?"

I imagine Marisa, all alone in the cargo-box office. If she noticed something was wrong, she would have busted in already. Either she's still sleeping, or...or the cops already found her and arrested her.

Or...

No. There's no other or. I can't think like that.

I need to get out of here. I need to find her. And then we need to run.

"Listen, I know you've been through a lot," Cop #1 says. "But it's all over now. You're safe. You just have to open the door."

Yeah, fat chance.

I tune out his voice. I picture the space between my hands and *focus*.

My fingertips go numb. The buzzing spreads to my wrists, my elbows, my shoulders.

"And we'll take you back to the station," Cop #1 says. "We'll get you some warm clothes and hot chocolate. Doesn't that sound nice?"

"Brody." It's Cop #2, calling from across the cafeteria. "There's somebody here. They want to talk to the kid."

I can hear the scowl in Cop #1's voice when he says, "Who?"

"He says he's the kid's legal guardian. He says the kid'll listen."

Oh, no.

I don't have another legal guardian. It's always been just me and Marisa.

But only one person would make that claim, and I know who it is before I hear his brisk footsteps echoing on the linoleum.

Doctor Jonathan Heed.

BY THE TIME we arrive at the hospital, my power has started to come back. Not the sparks themselves, but the beginnings of them, the tingle in my fingers and the buzzing in my bones.

"Here we are," EMT #1 says, smiling, and opens the doors. I brace myself, expecting to see Them already there, surrounding the car, waiting for me.

But the parking lot is quiet and still.

"Whup," EMT #1 says, chuckling. "Can't forget this." He picks up my backpack from the storage area and sets it on the foot of the stretcher.

They wheel me through the emergency entrance. The waiting room is just as hushed as the parking lot, and the only reactions I get are a few glances and a cough.

They're not here yet. I still have time.

The EMTs stop to talk to the lady at the front desk, and my mind is spinning over what I'm supposed to do.

I have to get out of here.

I have to find Zahira and Aaron.

I have to go back to Suddence.

I focus on my sparks again, begging them to *please* come back, and this time the buzzing goes up to my forearms, and I manage a bug-sized spark before I melt back, already dizzy. The spark wasn't even bright.

Just stay calm, Dany. Just stay calm and wait. It's no good wasting your strength like this.

But it's hard to stay calm. Every time I see a car pull into the parking lot, my heart seizes. I'm expecting a line of black cars to pour in any minute now, and what would I do then? I'm useless without my sparks. I'm weak. I won't be able to get away.

"Hey, kid," EMT #1 says, while EMT #2 is still talking to Front Desk Lady. "It seems like the doctor is a little busy with something right now, so we're just going to get you into a room first, and get you onto a comfier bed." He smiles, like he wants to show nothing about this is scary, and I wish he would stop doing that. "How are you feeling? Does it still hurt the same? Still a two?"

I nod, even though it feels like my whole waist is on fire.

"Are you feeling dizzy at all? Nauseous?"

I shake my head, which sends the whole world spinning. By the time everything stops swirling around like the inside of a snow globe, the EMTs are wheeling me down the hospital hallway.

Outside the emergency room door, a car pulls into the lot, and my pulse stops.

White truck. Yellow stripes. Rectangular lightbulbs on the roof like a police car.

It's the security vehicle from Suddence.

"Wait," I say, but the EMTs roll me around a corner,

and the emergency room vanishes. I crane forward, my side screaming in pain. "Wait. Go back."

But EMT #1 only gently presses me back and promises it's going to be alright, and then I'm being wheeled into an elevator. I watch the doors close, my heartbeat pounding in my skull.

I need to get out. I need to go back.

I grab the strap over my chest, fumbling for the buckle, but the EMTs only pull my hands away and feed me their speech about how I'm safe and it's alright and there's nothing to be afraid of, and they don't understand. Zahira and Aaron might be out there. They're out there, and I have to get to them before *They* do.

The elevator reaches the second floor, and the EMTs roll me out.

"I have to go back down," I say. The panic is clear in my voice, but I don't care. "I need to go back. Just for a second."

EMT #1 says, "We need to let the doctor see you first, alright?"

No. It's not alright. I stare down at the straps again. I could unclip the one across my chest fast enough, but the EMTs will grab me before I can reach for the one over my thighs, and I've seen enough medical shows to know that once I get rowdy, they'll inject me with something to make me fall asleep, and I'll be useless, and They'll take me, and I'll never reach Suddence. *Never.*

Numbness creeps up my fingertips.

Come on, Dany.

The numbness begins to burn. Pins and needles. It crawls up my arms, up to my shoulders, spilling down my spine and filling my head. I glare at the buckles on the straps.

I need them to be gone.

I *want* them to be gone.

Snap!

The buckles explode, and I flinch back as bits of plastic fly. The EMTs yelp in surprise, slowing the stretcher. I kick the lifeless straps aside and roll off the side, but pain screams up my leg and I cry out, crumpling.

"Oh!" EMT #2 cries, reaching out to catch me. I scramble back, releasing another spark. It's meant to only be a jolt, a static shock just painful enough to make her let me go, but when she screams, I see that she's bleeding.

EMT #1 backs away, startled. EMT #2 is clutching her hand and wailing.

"I'm sorry," I say desperately. I didn't mean to hurt her. But I can't stay to make sure she's okay, or to explain, or to show that I really mean it. *I'm sorry*.

I scurry to my feet, grab my backpack, and run.

"Wait!" EMT #1 shouts, and I hear his footsteps as he chases after me. "Dany, stop!"

Gritting my teeth, I reach behind me and spark an empty stretcher across the hall. EMT #1 shouts as he crashes into it.

I drag myself into the elevator and jam the ground floor button, and as I cling to the railing for balance, I catch one last glimpse of EMT #1's panicked face between the closing doors.

THE MOMENT I hear Cop #1 step away from the door, I fling the chair away from the handle and spark the door open, sending it smashing across the hallway. Cop #1 hollers and skitters back, and I take the chance to book it.

Out of the corner of my eye, I see *Them*. People who work for the clinic. People who work for Doctor Heed. There are four of them, dressed in normal clothes like they're just regular people. Like they're harmless.

I race down the hall, but I don't get far before two pairs of hands clamp around me. I scream, kicking and thrashing as They haul me back. They can't take me. I won't let them.

They want to steal my power? They want to see it so badly?

Fine.

I scream, and a volley of sparks bursts around me. The people holding me cry out, their hands loosening, and I shove away, holding my burning hands out in case either of Them tries something again. They're both on the ground, cradling their arms, and I see drops of blood on the linoleum.

Cop #1 and Cop #2 startle back, reaching for their holsters. Instinctively, I swing my hands towards them.

"Stop!" Doctor Heed calls.

The two cops freeze. They haven't drawn their weapons yet, and I can tell they're confused. They don't understand the threat is *me,* that *I'm* the reason two grown men are squirming on the ground. And if I so much as see their fingers twitch on their guns, they'll be next.

"Dany," Doctor Heed says gently, coming towards me with his leftover goons. My hands are shaking, and I don't know if I can call another volley of sparks. I can barely take a step back without wavering. But still, I glare at him with the promise of violence, and that's enough to make him and his goons go still at the edge of the cafeteria.

Doctor Heed puts his hands up. Not a surrender, but to prove he means no harm. I haven't seen him in two years. That was back when I thought he was nice. He still *looks* nice, wearing a brown coat over a blue plaid shirt and khaki pants like he's just somebody's very kind, very normal uncle.

But I know it's all a front, and I won't fall

for it again.

"Dany," he says. "Just stay calm."

Something's wrong, something in that thick lullaby drawl, and it takes me a second to put it together. My name. He knows my name, my *new* name.

That's not possible.

"How did you know that?" I demand.

He shakes his head a little, frowning. "Know what?"

My eyes dart between him and his goons. "You called me Dany."

His expression loosens, his lips parted in an *Ah.* "Well. I know because we found this at the motel."

He takes out a small book from inside his coat, and I almost gasp.

My diary.

The idea of him reading it makes my skin feel like it's about to peel away in papery curls. The diary is *mine.* No one else is allowed to read it. Not even Marisa.

"Give it back." I want to sound mean and strong, but I sound like a chihuahua trying to bark down a wolf. Doctor Heed is still holding my diary, and I can't stand it being in his hands for another second. "Give it *back!*"

"Alright," he says, and he sounds calm in a way that makes me feel like I'm wrong for being so loud. I kick the feeling away and watch him slide the book across the floor. It stops a few steps away from me, and I pick it up as quickly as I can, keeping one hand pointing at him. I want to flip through it and make sure he didn't ruin it, but I don't want to take my eyes off of him.

"Sorry to say, but I did read it," he says.

I hold the diary tight to my chest like that might exorcize Doctor Heed's sliminess from it.

"It seems like Marisa hasn't been telling you everything."

"Shut up," I say, taking a step back. "I'm leaving."

"Dany..."

"I'm leaving!"

"Dany, she is lying to you."

This is the first time he sounds like anything other than a nice reasonable man, and it makes me stop. There's something like panic in his voice. Like he really, really needs me to listen.

"No, she's not," I say.

"She's lying."

"*You're* lying!" I shout. "You're just saying whatever you want so I would believe you! So I would go with you! So—"

"So I could cut you apart?"

I clamp my mouth shut, my chest still pumping from shouting. Why would he admit that?

"Dany," he says evenly, and I want him to *stop* saying my name. "Why would I cut you apart?"

"Take my power. Experiment on me. Make more of me. I don't—" *I don't know* is what I was about to say, but I don't need to tell him that. He's playing mind tricks on me. I can't let him win that easily.

Doctor Heed shakes his head slowly. His blue eyes are wide, like he can't believe the barbaric things I'm saying. "No," he says quietly. "No. No. You...you are *special.* That power you possess, we have never seen it before, and we will never see it again. We would not *waste* you like that."

He takes a step forward, and I take a step back, my hand wavering. "Don't," I warn.

He stays where he is, his hands still held up. "Back at the motel? That was quite something. The biggest sparks we'd ever seen. Could you do that before, Dany? Or was that the first time?"

My eyes dodge to the side, just for half of a half of a second. But it seems to answer his question. He nods like it makes a lot of sense, something dark and glistening in his eyes. Sadness.

"We wanted to help you," he says. "We wanted to train you. Make you stronger. That was always our goal."

I scrape out a laugh through my teeth. "No, it wasn't."

"It was," he says. "From the very beginning. When we saw what you kids could do, we knew we had to help. You couldn't go on in life without being able to control it. If you had stayed with us, you would have been able to call those big bright sparks within months of training. Maybe even weeks. And by now, you could have been *the* most powerful person anyone has ever known." He spreads his arms and laughs. A wheeze of a laugh. "Dany. Think about what you can do with that power. How many people you can help. How many people you can save."

I feel my heart tipping towards him, but I yank it back and shake my head. Lies. He would say anything to make me believe him.

But something wriggles in the back of my mind. I had thought the same thing. That if I had trained every day, I would already be powerful. I would already be unstoppable.

And that night, after we escaped from the motel, when I got so mad at Marisa for acting like I shouldn't have used my power, like it's a dangerous weapon I should never use...

I was angry because none of it was true. My power *saved* us.

"That was what *we* wanted," says Doctor Heed, the sadness creeping into his voice. "We planned it, for years and years. But Marisa always had a different idea."

I shake my head. He said *always,* as if Marisa was part of the planning, as if Marisa *worked* for him, but that's not true. She only met him because of Lilian. She only met him *after* I showed my power.

That's what she told me.

"She thought it would be too difficult, too time-consuming to train you kids. She proposed that once you showed your power—"

My heart is rattling in my chest. "No," I say.

"—that we should put you under. Cut you apart. Study your brains. Figure out where this power comes from and figure out how to replicate it."

"No!" I shout. "She wouldn't—she wouldn't—"

"And we did not like the idea," he says, raising his voice. "We tried to convince her otherwise, but she would not listen. She was putting together a team. She was ready to do it. But that day, that *day*. We told her we wouldn't do it. We all rejected her proposal. And she took you, and she ran."

I shake my head. I want to cover my ears. I don't want to hear any more of this.

"I feel for her," Doctor Heed presses on. "I understand her pain. She lost her folks. I lost my wife. But she went too far."

My pulse hitches. *Her parents.* "What are you talking about?"

"Her folks. They died in Suddence." He pauses. "She didn't tell you?"

I grit my teeth. I don't want to shake my head. I don't want to prove him right.

"Suddence," he says. "The town where she grew up. The town where you were born. Something terrible happened. It killed her parents. It made her sick. Everyone had to leave. But it gave you your power. You, and all the other kids like you. And I think, in her mind, she needed her parents' deaths to mean something, before her grief ate her alive."

"No," I say, shaking my head. "I don't believe you. She wouldn't."

"She didn't want your power to grow, did she?" Doctor Heed says, gently. "She was keen on keeping your power weak. To make sure you are never strong enough to fight back."

Hot tears are blurring my vision, and my outstretched hand is shaking uncontrollably now. I try to keep it steady, to push back on what Doctor Heed is telling me. I don't understand it. I don't understand it. Marisa wouldn't lie to me. She wouldn't.

"Where was Marisa taking you," Doctor Heed asks. "Did she ever tell you?"

My voice is weak, and it takes a few tries to say, "Out of the country."

"To where?"

"Where I'll be..." A sob crawls up my throat. "Where I'll be safe."

"No," he says. Sadly, like he doesn't want to tell me this, but someone has to. "Out of the country, where we won't be able to stop her."

"No," I say sharply, like it could cut through the lie. "No. She wouldn't."

"Why would you think that?"

"Because—" Because I know Marisa. Because she raised me. Because she would do anything to protect me.

But she lies, a voice inside me says. *You know she lies.* She lied about Lilian. She didn't tell me about her medicine. She didn't tell me about Suddence, about where I was from, about why she adopted me. She kept so much from me until she was forced to tell me. What else is she holding back? What else is she lying about?

What if Doctor Heed is telling the truth?

But I think of her crying in my arms, her soft and tear-broken *sorry.* The way we slept back-to-back since she got sick, how she pinky-promised me ice cream and french fries, how after the motel she hugged me and I hugged her and we laughed through our tears and she promised she would never lie to me again. She wouldn't lie to me about this. She *wouldn't.*

A gunshot blasts through the school, and we all dodge. The bullet shatters a classroom window. The cops and Doctor Heed's goons whip out their guns and whirl around, firing back, and I see someone duck behind the wall.

Marisa.

"Stop," I say, but my voice is still weak. "Stop. Stop it!"

I thrust out my hand, and sparks burst against the cops and Doctor Heed's goons, knocking them aside. Doctor Heed, huddling behind a column, turns to look at me with eyes wide with betrayal.

Marisa takes this chance to shoot him in the shoulder.

He screams, clutching his wound, and I stagger back, my head spinning. He's on the ground, helpless, and Marisa is...Marisa is...

She's marching towards me, a gun in her hands and menace in her eyes.

"Marisa," I say. I'm backing away, without really meaning to. "I...I..."

"We have to go," she says, catching my wrist. She's still pale from sickness, and her hand is fever-hot around my arm. For a second, I dig my heels into the ground.

She looks back. "Dany?" She sees my expression, the tears slipping down my cheeks. "Dany, what did he tell you?"

"He..." I can't find the strength to speak. When I open my mouth again, I begin to cry.

"Listen to me." She cups the side of my face with her free hand. "You cannot believe anything he says. He will do anything to get you back. You understand? You cannot believe him."

How much of what he said is true? I want to ask.

How much of what you said is a lie?

But I only nod. A flutter of a nod. More tears trace down my cheeks, hot and scalding.

"Good," she says, and takes my wrist again. "Let's go."

THE ELEVATOR TAKES a billion years to reach the ground floor. The doors open with a ding, and I shove past two nurses to get out. Past the hallway, past the emergency room. I burst out into the cold, dark parking lot. My eyes fly over the cars until I see the white security vehicle, its blinkers flashing as it pulls out of the lot.

"Wait!" I shout, but the car doesn't stop. It slips onto the road, and soon, it'll be gone.

I hurry after it, even though I know it's impossible for me to catch up, even if I didn't hurt my ankle and my side wasn't three second away from bursting. I stop, gasping, watching as the car picks up speed.

I can't let it get away.

I clench my fists. Fire rushes up my arms, and I hurl my sparks at the car's tires.

There's an assault of sounds. Tires rupturing. Brakes screeching. A horrible *crunch!* as a car rams into the security vehicle from behind. Metal and plastic clattering across the pavement.

My shoes on the ground as I run over. My hard,

uneven breaths.

The security vehicle's back windows are tinted. I can't tell if Zahira and Aaron are inside, but I can see the guard in the front, holding his neck as he peels off the steering wheel. I march right up to the back door and spark it open.

Zahira and Aaron aren't here.

I slam the door shut and spark open the driver's door. The guard yelps, flinching back. The surprise in his eyes mixes with confusion when he sees me, an eleven-year-old kid with blood-stained clothes and eyes flashing with absolute murder.

"Where are they?" I demand.

The guard stares at me, his jaw hanging open.

"Where are they?"

He stammers. "I—they—I was told to drop them off here. Somebody came to get them."

"Who?" I say, and when he stumbles for an answer, I spark the door right off its hinges. *"Who?"*

"Doctor Heed!" he cries, terrified. "Someone named Doctor Heed!"

I was expecting the name, but it still sends a cold knife through my chest.

"Where did they go?" I say. The guard whimpers, and I gnash. "It's the last question. Where did they go?"

"In the hospital," he quavers. "That's all I know. I swear."

I spin back towards the hospital, leaving the guard cowering in the car. A few responders are rushing towards the accident. I slip past them, limping as fast as I can back to the emergency room.

Zahira and Aaron are here.

And They're here, too.

I stop at the entrance, catching my breath and holding my side. I don't feel any blood through the new bandages yet, but I know it won't be long before the pain becomes so unbearable that I pass out again. My eyes are already turning black at the edges, and I blink them away furiously.

Not now, Dany. You can't give up now.

I scan the room. Zahira and Aaron aren't here.

"Um, excuse me?" somebody says, and I look over. Front Desk Lady is staring at me, wide eyes flitting to the dried blood on my side.

"I'm looking for someone," I say, straightening. "A woman wearing pink. And a guy, wearing a blue hoodie. They're here. They were just here."

"Um," she says uncertainly, still eyeing the blood.

"I need to know *now!*" I insist. "They're in danger!"

That spurs her into action. "One of the meeting rooms," she says, pointing down the hall. "One of the empty ones. C or A, I can't remember." Her eyes go to my side again. "Do you need some help? Do you want me to call somebody?"

"No," I say. "Thank you."

And then I run.

DOCTOR HEED'S WORDS rattle in my head, echoing like a pebble dropped in a metal tank as Marisa drags me along.

You're lying, my own voice echoes with his. *She wouldn't.*

But everything he said makes sense.

Too much sense.

Why Marisa didn't like how powerful my sparks are getting.

Why Marisa wouldn't tell me about her past.

Why Marisa lied about so much.

I try to remember. Where is she taking me? I must have asked. At some point, I must have asked. But the more I dig through my memories, the more the truth sinks in.

I never asked. I never questioned her. About any of it. Not until this past week.

Because I trusted her.

I start to go numb, but not in the fiery way

of when I call my sparks. Truly numb. The world is a blur in my eyes, and my legs are suddenly heavy, and I can't breathe. Everything is too much. Doctor Heed's words in my head and the shouting behind us and the burning in my lungs and Marisa's fingers around my wrist.

I double over, the bottoms of my shoes dragging on the linoleum. My wrist breaks away from Marisa's grip, and she turns back, startled.

"Dany," she starts to say.

A gunshot, like the universe breaking in half. I scream, covering my head, and Marisa cries out.

She stumbles. Falls.

There's blood on her side.

Do something, Dany. Do something.

Marisa is hurt.

Marisa, who protected me all my life.

Marisa, who might be the one who wants to cut me apart.

"Hold your fire!" Doctor Heed shouts. No more gunshots come.

I break out of my trance and hurry to Marisa's side. She's clutching her ribs, her fingers staining red.

Footsteps. Doctor Heed.

"Dany," Marisa warns, and pushes me aside. She fires two shots down the hall, and Doctor Heed and his goons cuss and dive for cover. Marisa grabs my arm and shoves open the nearest door, hauling us both in.

I scramble as far as I can from the door. It's a small room, a broom closet, and it only takes a few scurries for my back to hit a clutter of cleaning tools in the corner. I huddle there, covering my head, knowing I should stop cowering, knowing I should stop *hiding.* I call for my sparks, but the order gets lost in the snowstorm in my head, and I can't stop shaking, can't stop crying.

The door knob rattles. I know it won't take long for Doctor Heed to break it down.

Come on, Dany. Do something.

But my eyes land on Marisa, and the order scatters again.

"Dany." Marisa crawls over, still holding her ribs. "Listen to me. Remember everything we talked about?"

I stare at her through my tears. Her sickly pale skin. The blood spreading on her coat. The fire in her eyes, despite it all.

The door knob stops rattling. "Dany," Doctor Heed says. "Open the door."

"Is it true?" I say. "What he said? That you— that it was you who wanted to—"

"Dany." She holds my shoulder tight. "You can't listen to him."

"He said it was you who wanted to cut me apart," I say, my voice splintering. "He said you were taking me somewhere...somewhere..."

"Dany," Doctor Heed says outside. "I know it

isn't easy to break away from her. She tricked you good. But you know what's right, Dany. You know she's lying to you."

"Dany," Marisa says, and I feel like she and Doctor Heed are pulling me between them, pulling until I break. "Dany, I...I..."

But her words bleed away, and I can see shame in her eyes. Guilt.

I shrink away.

"Dany," she says, eyes filling with tears. "Dany, there's a lot I didn't tell you. There's a lot I couldn't...I didn't..." She sobs. A gasp of a sob. "But I swear. I *swear.* I never wanted to cut you apart. I saw what he did to the other kids. Doctor Heed was going to turn you into something you do not want to be. I had to get you away."

"Dany," Doctor Heed says outside, and I cover my head, wishing I could shrivel away into nothing.

"Listen to me," Marisa says. "Listen. You remember everything we talked about, right?"

Without lifting my head, I nod, gritting back my sobs.

"Then you run. I'll boost you up to the window. I'll keep them distracted here. Understand?"

Window. I didn't even notice a window. I picture myself climbing out of it, dropping in the snow, running. Alone.

"Dany, do you understand?"

Slowly, I look up at her, my cheeks damp with

tears. Doctor Heed made Marisa sound like a person who only cares for her own goals. A person who doesn't care about me. A person who is selfish.

A selfish person wouldn't sacrifice themselves. Not like this.

There's something Marisa isn't telling me. There's something real in what Doctor Heed told me. I don't know which parts of their stories are true, or which parts are false.

But I can't let them kill Marisa.

I can't just let her die.

She's everything. She's *everything*. She took care of me. She protected me. She knows me and she loves me and she holds me when I cry and I need her. I need her.

"No," I say. "I'm not leaving you."

"I'm hurt," she insists. "I'm sick. I can't come with you."

"No." I dive into her arms, clinging hard to her. "I can't. I need you. I don't want to leave you."

"Dany—"

"Cardinal rule," I say through my sobs. "We stay together. We stay *together.*"

I clench my fists. I call for my sparks. We have to fight our way out of this. I have to be strong.

But my power is a weak ripple in my hands, and when They break down the door and tear Marisa away, all I can do is scream.

I SHOVE OPEN the door to Meeting Room A.

Empty.

I stagger to Meeting Room C and twist the handle.

Locked.

In the emergency room, I can hear Front Desk Lady calling for security. I shouldn't have told her there's danger. I'm running out of time.

I step back and thrust out my hand. Sparks blast the knob into smithereens, and I slam the door open.

Zahira is sitting on one side of the meeting table. She flinches back and stares at me, her eyes overflowing with tears and surprise.

I turn to the other side of the table.

Lilian.

She stands up so quickly her chair clatters back. "Dany—"

I send sparks exploding before her, and she crashes back. Zahira cries out, scrambling to her feet, and when she looks at me, her eyes are filled with horror. Just like that night, when I saved her in the alley.

"Dany," she begins, in a wavering voice.

I say, "We have to go."

I turn and march back down the hall. Behind me, I hear Zahira hurrying to follow.

"Wait," she says. "Wait, Dany, you're hurt."

"It doesn't matter," I grit out. "You're driving."

"But..." she stammers. "Aaron—he was hurt, and they took him—"

"We don't need him."

"Dany—"

I march out the emergency entrance and search the parking lot for JJ's blue car, but of course it isn't here. It's still in Suddence, at the edge of the endless pit, broken and dead. I remember Zahira's promise to bring it back before JJ's date, and despite the pain in my leg and my side, the broken promise is the one that hurts the most. I did this. It's my fault.

But this will all be over soon. Just a few more hours, and I'll be out of their lives forever.

We're halfway across the parking lot when I hear a van door sliding open. Two of Them melt out from between the cars and block our way. I pull back to release a volley of sparks, but behind me, Lilian shouts, "Dany!"

Zahira whirls around to face her, but I keep my glare pinned on the goons in front of us.

"Get out of my way," I warn.

I hear Lilian stepping closer, limping slightly. "Dany," she says. Pleads. "We can talk about this, alright? You're hurt. You've been through a lot. I know you're scared, but I won't hurt you."

"Dany," Zahira whispers.

I ball my fists. "Tell them to get out of my way," I call back.

Lilian lets out an exasperated breath. "Dany…"

"Tell them to get out of my way," I say again, harder, sharper. I raise my hands, and the goons falter back. "You know what I can do."

The parking lot goes silent, but everything is pulled taut. The roar of blood in my ears. The prickling numbness clawing up my arms. The goons' eyes flickering between me and my hands. My seething breaths, my heart thundering in my chest. All of it, pulled tight, ready to snap. Someone has to let go, and it isn't going to be me.

And Lilian says, "Let them go."

The goons look at her with surprise. She takes a wavering breath and says, "It's okay. Let them go."

The goons back off. I watch them, making sure they aren't planning to try anything, before I step forward, heading for their van. Zahira lingers behind, still looking at Lilian, and I grab her sleeve and drag her along. She doesn't fight, not really, but her boots catch on the pavement like she doesn't want to come.

I peer through the van's window. The key is still in the ignition.

We get in the car, and I keep my eyes on Lilian through the windshield. She's still standing at the emergency entrance, looking at me with pleading in her eyes. Behind her, the security guards are finally arriving, staring confused at the scene.

"Go," I tell Zahira, and she starts the engine.

We peel out of the lot. My eyes stay on Lilian, watching her resigned figure get smaller and smaller.

And then we turn a corner, and she's gone.

"NO!"

Marisa is screaming, trapped behind a tangle of arms, reaching out to me desperately. I scamper to my feet and catch her wrist, but then arms are circling around me too, dragging me out of the broom closet.

"No!" I scream again, kicking, crying. Doctor Heed stands between us as we are pulled apart. "No!"

My power runs in a hot shudder up my arms, so sudden my mind blazes white. With a cry, I spark the hands holding me. I ignore the bellows of pain behind me and the bruising shocks up my knees when I land on the ground. I pull my focus towards Marisa, but Doctor Heed is in my way, running towards me, reaching out to grab me—

I throw out my hands.

I want him to be *gone*.

A burning flash of light. A hard bang of

thunder.

Doctor Heed screams.

I don't know what I did to him. I see spots of red, the white of his teeth as he screams, but he's already falling to his knees, and my eyes are on Marisa.

I gather my fists, concentrating on the hands holding her tight.

Crack!

The goons cry out, letting Marisa go. She sprawls, screaming as she clutches her ribs.

"Marisa!" I run for her, dizziness bleeding into my brain, making me stumble. She manages to push onto her hands, and then to her feet. There are blots of red where the goons were holding her, and I don't know if it's Their blood, or if I hit Marisa by accident, but she's free now, and we're running, reaching for each other—

Bang!

Marisa screams.

"No!" I hurry to catch her as she falls. Her thigh is bleeding, the red already soaking down to her knee.

Hands grab me from behind, pulling me away, pulling us apart. Marisa cries out in pain when They haul her to her feet, and I scream. *Let her go! Stop it! Let her go!* All a roar in my ears, blurred shrieking, melding with a terrible buzz, filling my head, filling my body. *You're hurting her! Stop it! Let her go!*

I reach out for her. Her fingers almost touch mine.

And then a bag comes down over my head, and they're taking her away, and my screams become wordless. Fire rises up my arms, engulfing my whole body, pain and pins and needles and a single word searing through my brain—

BURN.

WE DRIVE FOR a long, long time before Zahira finally says, quietly, "Dany."

I let out an uneven breath. The pain in my side is horrible, even though I took the last of my medicine, but if I don't move, if I don't talk, if I just sit here and think about anything other than the hot iron poke melting through my spleen, I can grit my teeth through it.

"Dany."

"What?" I say a little too sharply.

She keeps her eyes on the dark road. "That woman," she says slowly. "Lilian Heed. She told me—"

"Don't believe anything she says." I wrap my arms tight around myself and goddamn wish she would just leave it at that.

She goes quiet. For about ten seconds, it's just the scrape of tires on asphalt and the rush of the grey, dead farmlands passing by as we ride down a long country road.

Then she says, "It's not just what she told me."

I close my eyes and focus on taking deep breaths. You're almost there, Dany. Just hang on.

"In the car," Zahira says. "When the security guard was taking us to the police station. Lilian, she called the guard. She…" She shakes her head, frowning a little. "She said she doesn't want to press charges against us. She told him to bring us to the hospital instead, and she…she asked to talk to us. And she explained. Everything."

I huff out a laugh. "And you believed her?"

"That's not just it," Zahira says. "When we got to the hospital, she took one look at Aaron and made sure a doctor looked at his eye."

"So?"

"So—so you said They would have killed us. I was expecting it. I was *terrified* in the backseat of that car, and I kept trying to figure out how we were going to get out of this." She sits back with more force than necessary. Her knuckles are white around the steering wheel. "You make Them sound like the devil, but Lilian had every chance to do something to us, and she didn't. She could have told the guard to take us literally anywhere else. She could have left the charges on us and just let us rot in jail. She could have just shoved us into one of her vans the moment we got to the hospital. But she didn't. She—"

"That's just what she does!" I say, close to shouting. "She plays all these tricks on you. Pretending to be nice. You can't just trust her because she's nice."

"She told me Doctor Heed died two days ago. In the high school."

Everything in me is burning. I don't know what she wants me to say to that.

"Dany, you knew that, didn't you?"

I grind my teeth. I guess it's clear what my answer is because she barks out a mean, unhappy laugh.

"You told me he's after you. But he's dead, and you knew, but you..." She laughs again, and this time, her anger is clear. "Why would you lie to me about that? Why didn't you just tell me?"

"Doctor Heed, Lilian, it doesn't matter," I snap. "They all want the same thing. I just didn't want to make it so freaking complicated."

"No, Dany, *this* is. *This* is more complicated. I just— I don't understand. Why can't you just give me straight answers? Why is it always these half truths and bloody labyrinths?"

My fists are gathered so tight they hurt. "What's your point?"

"My point is that your story doesn't add up!" she shouts. "This whole time, you're trying to reach someone in Suddence all on your own so they can help you, but Lilian is right there! You—" She bites back anger in her voice, though it's still boiling in her eyes. In a low, barely steady voice, she says, "Is there even someone waiting for you in Suddence?"

I point my burning eyes out the window.

"Dany, look at me." The fury is creeping back into her tone. "Is there even somebody there?"

I don't want to answer her. I don't want to look at her. I just want her to *drive*.

She slams on the brakes.

The force of it throws me forward. The seatbelt lurches me to a hard stop, and pain sears up my side.

The car skids to a halt and tosses me back against

the seat. I whirl on Zahira and say, "What the *hell?*"

She kills the engine and rounds on me, one white-knuckled hand still gripping the steering wheel. The headlights are still on, and in the yellowish light, the corners of her mouth are turned way, way down, and I know she's truly, thoroughly pissed.

"Tell me the truth," she says.

I meet her furious glare. "Or what?"

"Or I won't take you to Suddence!"

"Fine!" I fling off my seatbelt and thrash open the door. "Then I'll fucking *walk.*"

My ankle screams and wobbles the moment I put weight on it, but I manage not to fall. Walk? I want to run. I want to just get this over with so I don't have to worry about any of it anymore. So I don't—

"Dany!" The driver-side door clips open. "Dany!"

I ignore her.

I shouldn't have asked for her help.

I should have just walked. On my own, like it should be.

"Dany!"

"Just go away!" I shout. "Just turn around and go away! I don't need you anymore!"

But her heeled boots are still following me, and she's getting closer. My fingertips are starting to burn. Zahira calls my name again, and I say, "Go *away.*"

"No!" Her footsteps quicken. I can see her in the corner of my eye. "Dany. I got you this far. I deserve to know the *truth!*"

"You already know the truth!" I know I shouldn't be yelling. Not when I can't feel my fists anymore and fire is climbing up past my wrists and my temples are aching. I know. I *know,* but my chest feels like it's about to burst. "Go away. I don't want your help anymore. Just go. Go!"

"No—Dany—" She gnashes. "Dany, you're hurt! You're limping! Look at you, please—"

I make myself walk faster, gritting against the blinding pain in my leg and side. My head is starting to buzz, and the world is turning into static. The fire reaches my collarbones, splintering down my spine, and I know something bad is about to happen, and I need Zahira to *stop.*

"Dany!"

Stop.

"Please—"

Stop.

"Dany!"

"STOP!"

The world explodes.

Bright white sparks. In a flash, they're there, bursting against the empty fields around us, filling up the dark skies, flooding heat into the night. A thousand lightning bolts, striking all at once.

There, and then gone.

And then quiet. A quiet so sudden it makes me dizzy. Makes my ears ring. Makes the world collapse in on itself, swallowed into a black hole.

The same quiet that came after the flurry of wood and splinters, the pain across my cheek, the gash in my side. The same quiet when I opened my eyes and I was on the ground and the school was on fire and Marisa was— she was—

I whirl around. Zahira is huddling against the front of the van, shaking and frightened, but she's fine.

She's fine.

And the relief makes my legs dissolve, and I crumple to my hands and knees.

My heavy breaths make it through the muffle first. Then a sound like rain, pebbles and dirt falling back to the ground. Zahira's trembling gasps. The far, full rumble of the empty space around us. Miles and miles and miles.

Dizziness swarms me, and darkness bleeds into my vision, and my chest is lurching, trying to catch breath, but I say, "You want to know the truth?" I don't know if Zahira is listening. I don't know if she wants to hear it anymore. "It was me. At the high school. I…"

Crawling across the linoleum. Heat growing closer and closer. Marisa's blood on the ground, the char around her wound, the look in her eyes, the fear—

The scrape in my throat when I screamed. The tears falling down my cheeks, burning me more than the heat of the fire. I wanted to save her. I was trying to save her. What did I do? What did I do?

"I killed her." I don't know if I'm saying it out loud. I can't feel my mouth moving. "I killed her. I killed her." I can hear myself saying it now, and I look up to make sure Zahira hears it, too. She has to hear it. "I killed her, and I…"

Marisa tried to say something. She tried to say my name. She was shuddering, gasping for air, and I've never seen her so scared. I tried to hold her wound, and her fingers wrapped around mine so hard it hurt, but I held on. I held on and she tried to say my name again, through the blood on her lips, through her jagged, trembling breaths.

And then her hand was gone from my hand, and the light was gone from her eyes, and then she was gone. Just gone. And I still can't understand it. How a whole person could be gone. How she could be right in front of me but gone. How she could be right beside me all my life and just *gone.*

"I can't leave," I say, my voice small and shaking because my lungs are crushing in on themselves. And I'm crying, and I shouldn't be, because it was *me.* It was me who killed her. "I can't leave her. I can't leave her." I clutch the front of my shirt, where Marisa's key is looped around my neck. It's heavy again, burning. "I can't just leave her. I need to bury her. I need to..." I squeeze my eyes shut and swallow the sob tearing up my throat. "I just need to take her to Suddence. I just need to take her back."

And then I just cry,

I hear the scratch of Zahira getting off the ground. She's leaving. She'll drive away, and I'll be alone. Somehow, the word comforts me. Alone. My tears drain away, and the weight is gone from my shoulders.

It's just me now.

On my own, as it should be.

But when I open my eyes, she's still here. Standing in front of the van, dark eyes running with tears. Looking at me.

She says, "Come on."

I stare at her with blurry eyes. "What?"

She tips her head towards the car. "Come on. Let's

go."

I wipe my eyes. My lungs are still gasping with sobs. "Go where?"

"I'm taking you to Suddence."

It takes a few seconds for the words to really sink in. I sniff and wipe my eyes again. "You're supposed to be mad at me."

"I am," she says. Sharp, like the snap of a branch. "I'm goddamn furious, and you lied to me, and…" Tears slip down her cheeks, and she angrily scrubs them away with the flat of her hand. "You're just a kid. God, Dany, you're just a *kid*. You're supposed to be going to school and hating math and playing four squares with your friends. But you're—"

Her voice catches, and she covers her eyes, swaying on her feet. When she lowers her hands, her eyes are still wet with tears, but there's a blaze of determination, too.

"So," she says. "I'm taking you to Suddence. But you have to promise me one thing." She marches over, still brushing at her tears. "When you finish whatever it is you're doing there, I'm taking you back to the hospital. You're going back to Lilian, and you're going to let her help you. You're going to find somewhere safe to live, and you're going to have a normal life. Got it?"

I stare at her, lightheaded and faint.

Normal life.

She offers me her hand, and I take it, letting her pull me to my feet. The world sloshes around me, but Zahira holds me steady. I remember Marisa's hand tight around mine, and now mine are tight around Zahira's. A lifeline. A last hope.

Zahira helps me limp back to the car. I slump in the seat, dizzy and out of breath. My side burns, through the fuzziness of it all, and when I press my hand against it, I feel something warm and wet.

"Zahira," I say. She stops in the middle of the closing the door. I should tell her we need to turn around. I need to go to the hospital. I'm hurt.

But I say, "Thank you."

She smiles, just a little, and somehow that feels better than if she had said anything at all.

She gets into her side of the car and starts the engine, and with a rising haze of purple where the sky meets the ground, we drive towards Suddence.

SOMEWHERE.

Somewhere out there I can feel cold air stinging my skin. My shoes scraping along the snowy sidewalk. Wetness on my hands. My blood. Marisa's blood. There's pain. Somewhere. Everywhere.

Behind me, the orange light grows. The faint crackle of fire, the stink of smoke.

In my pocket, Marisa's phone is ringing.

I sink to my knees. Everything is suddenly so heavy. The clothes on my skin, the air in my lungs. My backpack hanging from my shoulders, Marisa's bag clutched against my chest. I want to lie down. I don't want to carry anything anymore.

The phone is still ringing.

Numbly, I slip out Marisa's cellphone. The caller ID doesn't show a name. I pick it up.

"Marisa?" says the voice on the other end. "Marisa, are you alright?"

Lilian. I can tell, even though she's all shaky with panic. I open my mouth. I want to answer. But I can't make a sound.

"Are you there?" Lilian says. "Marisa?"

I slump forward, closing my eyes.

Not Marisa. Marisa isn't here.

Marisa is dead.

A long silence later, she says, "Dany?"

I stop breathing. For a moment she sounded just like Marisa.

"Dany," she says again, slower. "Is that you?"

I take a breath to answer, but my throat closes up, and I'm crying.

"Dany, where's Marisa?" Panic creeps back into her voice. "I heard—where's Marisa? What happened? Dany?"

"She's..." My voice cracks, tumbles, scatters. "She's..."

Lilian is quiet. When she speaks again, she's urgent. "Where are you, Dany? Are you safe?"

Don't tell her, a little voice says. *She's one of Them.*

But Marisa said. She said.

Last resort.

"Driveway," I say. "School." I'm not sure if the words make it past my mouth. I try again, but it comes out weaker, and I fall into tears.

"Okay," she says, and I hear rustling. "Okay, stay there, Dany, alright? Just stay there. I'm coming to get you. I'll get you somewhere safe. Just stay right there."

I let my hand slip down to my lap, Lilian's voice still chittering, begging for an answer. I can feel the heat of the fire on my back. I can hear sirens in the distance.

Stay right here. Stay right here while Marisa disappears inside the school.

It's okay, Dany. It's over now. Lilian is coming to get you, and she'll protect you, and you'll go somewhere safe and...

And...and...and...

And what?

Move on? Go to school? Have a normal life?

Pretend like none of this ever happened?

I remember sitting in the empty cafeteria, trying to imagine myself eating and talking with my friends. I remember the deep ache in my heart because I wanted this life, but it isn't mine. *This* is. Taking it day by day, never stopping. I panicked when I pictured living on the road with Marisa for the rest of my life. That wasn't the future I wanted, but it's the only one I can imagine, and now she's gone, and I don't know what I'm supposed to do. Oh, god, what am I supposed to do?

I push onto my feet, swaying, dizziness eating into my eyesight.

The sirens are getting close.

I can't stay here.

I take a step, holding tight to my side. I don't know where to go. The world is suddenly so big and dark and it's going to swallow me alive.

But I can't leave Marisa here.

One foot in front of the other. Walking. Biting through my pain.

And then I run.

I run and I run and I run.

MY MIND DRIFTS awake when Zahira gently shakes my shoulder.

"Hey," she says. "We're here."

I slowly open my eyes. I don't remember falling asleep. For a moment I'm not sure where *here* is, and the cloud is slow to leave my mind.

Suddence. We're here.

I sit up a little straighter. The world is brighter now, soft and peachy from the dawn. The town doesn't look so scary now. Just lost, and lonely, and somewhere in my cottony mind I'm glad I'm here when it's morning.

"Where are we going?" she asks.

It takes a second to put together what she's asking. I press my fingers to the key, trying to remember the number. "109," I say. "House 109."

We wind through the neighbourhood. I watch the passing houses, dyed pink in the dawn, and imagine living here. But what I picture is me and Marisa in our little townhouse, old and cozy and ours.

Zahira stops in front of #109 and helps me out of the

car. I have to hold my side tightly now, but when she asks, I tell her I'm alright. It doesn't hurt too much. I'll be okay.

She helps me up the steps to the front door. My hands shake as I gather the key from under my hoodie. I'm standing where Marisa once stood, holding a key she once held, and the thought makes me a little dizzy.

I slide the key in the lock, my heart skipping hard and heavy, and when the door unlocks, the relief makes me a little dizzy, too.

I manage to step in on my own. The entryway is small, like the townhouse we used to live in. The place is covered in dust. I can see it floating in the weak rays of sun shining through the windows.

In the dining room, a chair is knocked over, a plate shattered on the ground. But otherwise, the house is peaceful, glowing in the morning sun. Like nothing was ever wrong.

"Upstairs," I say, and Zahira comes to help me up the steps. Pictures line the stairway wall. Marisa, younger. Her parents. A dog.

I reach for a photo of Marisa with her parents at the town's grand opening. A big bright banner says, *Welcome to Suddence!* and balloons line the street. Before everything went wrong. When they were still happy.

"You want the picture?" Zahira asks, and I nod. She takes it down for me. I brush the dust off of it and look closer at Marisa. It's strange seeing her as a kid, with messy hair and freckles and bandages on her knees and a wide smile showing off her pink braces. I don't understand it. I don't think I ever will.

On the second floor, Marisa's door is marked with a

hand-drawn sign and instant camera photos of her dog, a big golden retriever. I take one of them. I wish I knew the dog's name.

"Should we go in?" Zahira says, her hand hovering over the golden knob.

I nod.

She opens the door. My eyes land on the bed. The blanket has patterns on it. I don't know why that's the first thing I notice. Rocket ships and stars and moons. The bed is unmade, and the carpet is messy with paper and cardboard.

I step in, taking in Marisa's childhood room. The white dresser and small desk and round mirror surrounded by pictures of her friends. Trinkets line a shelf filled with books. Marisa likes to read. When we're hiding in motels, she's always reading. I don't know what her favourite book is. I never thought to ask.

I stop in the middle of the messy carpet. There's a half-finished card by my foot. The construction paper lettering isn't done, but clearly it was supposed to say *Happy Anniversary,* and underneath it is a pencil sketch of her parents.

I close my eyes. The world is swimming.

"Dany?" Zahira says, lingering near the door.

I let go of a small, skittering breath. "I'm okay."

I collect the card and the pictures around the mirror. With a hard blink, I realize one of the photos is Lilian. She looks so different, with glasses and pimples and fuzzy hair tied in two buns.

Tentatively, Zahira says, "Do you need anything else?"

I shake my head. I can't bear being in this room for another second.

"What now?"

I feel sick. I want to lie down in Marisa's bed, curl up and never wake up.

But it's almost over.

Now, I bury her.

I tell Zahira to take me to the backyard, where the grass is up to my waist and the trees are leafless in the cold winter air. I ask her to dig a hole for me, just a small one, and she leaves me on the back porch steps so she can find a shovel in the garden shed.

I unshoulder my backpack and take out the candy tube. Carefully, I lay out what's inside.

A special coin I was going to give Marisa for her birthday, with a little rabbit on it.

A lock of my hair, the part she dyed for me.

The charm on her cellphone, a scuffed cartoon cat, taken before I threw the phone in the river.

Lastly, from the side pocket of my backpack, I take out her sunglasses, which I found in her purse after the high school, and I leaned over it and cried and cried.

This is all I have left of her.

"Dany," Zahira says. She's dusting the dirt off her hands, a hole in the grass by her feet. I bring everything over, along with what I collected from the house. I bury what I can in the tiny hole, and the rest of it, the framed picture and the card and her sunglasses, I leave around it like offerings. At last, I slip the key from around my neck and lay it in the circle of bare dirt. I keep my hand there, trying to think of what to say.

I love you, I think hollowly. *Good bye.*

And then it's done.

I wait. I don't know what I'm waiting for. Maybe I thought if I buried her, if I finally let her go, I would feel better. I would feel peace. I would feel some kind of surge, some kind of need to keep going, that I'm free now, that I can move on. Different. Different, somehow.

But kneeling here, looking at the little patch of dirt in the grass, all I can think is one thing.

Marisa's gone.

She's really gone now.

Pain twists in my chest, but I don't have the strength to cry anymore. A dry sob escapes, and then it's like all the air goes out of me. I sag over, pressing my head to my hands, and what I really want to say comes tumbling out.

I'm sorry.

I'm sorry.

Come back.

The world goes numb, shifting and swaying. Across the sea, I hear Zahira saying my name, and there's worry in her voice, but the pain in my side is a roar of blood in my ears, and I'm not sure where I am anymore. Somewhere warm. Somewhere cold. Somewhere where the pain is shards of ice prickling through every cell in my body, and breathing feels like drinking molten-hot metal. Somewhere where I'm floating, and nothing matters anymore.

"Dany." Zahira drifts over me in a ring of darkness, like I'm sinking down a well. "Dany, hang on."

She lifts me up, and I feel her running.

A car door slams shut. I'm lying in the backseat. The

engine starts, but it stalls and stalls and stalls.

"Just hang on," Zahira calls over the sound. "Dany, just hang on."

It's okay, I want to tell her.

This is what I wanted, anyway.

I could never picture myself growing up.

My life ends here. It ends on the road.

The engine starts, the sound rumbling through me, and I close my eyes.

Marisa is driving through the night. When I wake up in the morning, I'll be in the next motel, tucked away in bed. Marisa will bring me breakfast. I'll turn on the TV, flip through the channels, hoping this stillness will last.

When I wake up, I'll be with her.

PART V:
Stay Together

Dear Dany.

It's strange talking to you like this. Since you're reading this, you must be all better.

Just so you know, I stayed as long as I could. I felt like I had to be there when you woke up so you wouldn't be scared and confused. But Lilian told me to go home. There was nothing I could do here. But mostly, I think she was worried about Them regrouping and coming after you again. She didn't want me caught up in the mess. It's funny. This whole time I thought I was already caught up in the mess.

She said I could send letters, though, so here we are. Hi. How are you. I hope the hospital food isn't as shitty as they say.

What's up with me? Well. They paid me a lot of money to keep quiet. Like, _a lot_ of money. I would have kept my mouth shut even without the cash. Shh, don't tell them that. The money paid for JJ's busted car. It also paid for mine. Thank god I got to her before the shop smashed her for parts. She has a name, by the way. I don't think I ever told you that. It's Shirley.

well, here I am at the bottom of the page. Until next time!

-Zahira.

Dear Dany,

Hi. It's been a while. Sorry. I was busy moving back in with my family. It's just for now, until I can get my footing again. I'm not sure if I'm going to go back to med school or not. You and I really went on a hell of a road trip, huh?

I can't really talk to my family about what happened, though, so I have to try really, really hard to pretend I'm not messed up. At least Lilian got us a therapist to talk to. Oh, by "us" I mean me and Aaron. If you're worried we might be back together, don't be. We're not dating again, and probably never will. But we're friends. Well, "friends." We're on friendly terms. But it's good to be able to talk about what happened to someone, even if he wasn't there for all of it.

I didn't mean to make this letter a bummer. Here's a picture of Poquito.

Aaron named him. It means "a little bit" in Spanish because Poquito really was so tiny when we got him. He's a Pomeranian! At least, we're pretty sure he is.

That's it for now, I guess. Khoda hafez! It means good-bye in Farsi.

-Zahira.

Dear Dany,

Hello! Hope you're doing well. Life has been a lot lately. I got a job. Remember when I told you I used to work in a pizza place? Yeah. Back there again. They changed names, but it's in the same place, so I can still see that arcade I told you about. I still think about it, by the way, you using your ~sparks~ to cheat the games. If you ever end up trying it and it works, <u>please</u> let me know.

So I'll be busy working for…I don't know. The foreseeable future. Aaron got a job too, so at least neither of us will be moping around too much. He's doing part time at the car shop or something. Jealous. I'm working full-time. At least I get to take the leftover pizzas home.

Bye-bye for now!

-Zahira.

Dear Dany,

I tried one of the machines at the arcade. I swear they rig these things. They got these huge claw machines set up, and I've been watching the kids play. That claw is definitely loose. These kids are getting swindled.

I met up with Aaron and JJ the other day. Hard to believe it's been two months since everything happened. It feels like it's been a hundred years, but it also feels like it was just last week. I forgot to mention: Aaron and I had to tell him the made-up version of the truth. I felt so bad about it because we messed up his car and ruined his plans. I felt like we owed him the truth. But I also know the danger of letting the real story slip. Plus, I signed a contract. So that's that.

Anyway, he forgives us for wrecking his car,

and that was before we told him we could pay for it. He's just relieved we're okay. Even though we thought we ruined his plans, apparently he still managed to go on that date by convincing his date to come pick him up. Two-hour drive! I think we call that dedication.

That's what's going on with us so far. I'm still at my pizza job. Aaron's doing full-time now. I wish there was a way for me to know what's going on with you. I noticed you had a TV in your room. I hope they play some good movies on there.

That's it for now. Hello from all three of us!
-Zahira.

THERE'S A KNOCK at the door, and Lilian comes in with a smile and a lunch tray.

"Morning," she says, even though it's almost twelve. "Time for lunch."

It's still a little strange to think about Lilian as a good guy. I try to sit up straighter, but I still feel like my body is going in slow motion. And I'm still so weak that I need about three pillows to help me stay sitting.

Lilian comes over to help me. The bed is already angled up as much as it can go, so she just readjusts the pillows and punches them into the right shape.

I stare down at the lunch tray she put on the table. I'm sure the food tastes good. They're colourful and steaming hot, and there's a blob of green jelly on the side. But my appetite is still somewhere in the garbage.

The spoon wobbles dangerously when I pick it up, but I stick it stubbornly into the macaroni. All last month Lilian had to feed me, and I don't think I can stand it anymore.

I can feel her laser eyes on me as I scoop the noodles up. She says, "How are you feeling today?"

I make a bunch of sounds through my food that translates to *bad, but better than yesterday, I guess,* which Lilian seems to get, which is good because I don't really feel like talking right now.

She didn't arrange for me to have the room to myself. I guess she thought that would be too conspicuous. I share the room with two other kids who hog the tiny TV all day and watch cartoons. Luckily, they're both off doing some group activity that I'm definitely not well enough to join yet, so I get to watch basketball. Because my brain is so foggy, sometimes I find myself trying to spark the ball into the net. It's a good thing I'm still too weak to call up anything, or I would have accidentally smashed the TV already.

"What team are we rooting for?" Lilian asks.

I shrug. I haven't decided yet.

I manage half of the macaroni before I start feeling sick. I skip the soup and go straight for the jelly before my body tries to convince me it's a good time to throw up.

"Guess what?" Lilian says with a small smile.

I frown, trying to remember if it's some special date. It could be. I keep forgetting what day it is. Being in a sepsis-induced coma for weeks does that to you. "What?"

She shows me an envelope, and I drop my jelly spoon.

Zahira.

The first thing I did when I woke up—well, the first thing I did was panic weakly, but when the cracked-apart pieces of my mind finally came back together and I remembered the name of the long-haired, pink-jacketed woman, I begged to see her. I wanted to know she was okay. Lilian told me not to worry, but I *did* worry, but I was also too occupied with feeling like crap to do anything about it.

Mostly, I was afraid that after everything, Zahira wouldn't want anything to do with me anymore. I get it, though. I lied to her. I ruined her life. I ruined JJ's life. I even ruined his car. The weird part is, I was even worried about *Aaron*. He *did* drive me to Suddence. I can't not be at least a little grateful about that.

But then Lilian showed me all the letters that Zahira sent, and the relief nearly made me faint. She opened the letters for me and held them up so I could read them, and all I could think was, *We're okay.*

"I'll let you read it on your own, okay?" Lilian pats my arm. "I'll bring over some pen and paper."

She takes my half-eaten lunch away and leaves me staring at the envelope.

We're leaving in a few weeks. That's always been the plan. Once I get well enough to be discharged, Lilian will take me out of the country, to where she's hiding all the other kids like me, just in case They manage to regroup and try to come after us again.

It's still hard to wrap my head around there being other kids like me. I know Doctor Heed told me about them, when he said we would all go to summer camp together. But that whole time I thought they must have all been vivisected and died already, and after I found out the truth, that nobody actually wanted to cut me apart, I just...I never thought about it. I was only thinking about Suddence. I guess some part of me knew it didn't matter if there were other kids and if they were still alive. I was never going to meet them, anyway.

But Lilian had gotten them all out. Most of them, at least. She hadn't been lying when she said she didn't agree with Doctor Heed anymore. She hadn't been lying when she called Marisa and told her she wanted to get us out. She'd really wanted to help. And we hadn't believed her.

The whole "moving away" thing scares me a little. But what scares me more is that I would stop getting letters from Zahira. They're the only things keeping me afloat right now. It also doesn't help that the only letter I sent back was pretty crappy.

Dear Zahira,

Hi. As you can tell, I'm awake now. Hooray!

The hospital food isn't bad. They won't let me have ice cream though. I'm glad your car is alright. I hope you finally put some paint on the bald spots.

And then I didn't know what else to write and went to sleep and when I woke up, I added:

Poquito is so cute. Send me more pictures please.

What I really wanted to write was *I'm happy you're okay and you don't hate me and I wish you can come visit me.* What I ended up writing is:

Tell JJ I said hi. And punch Aaron for me.
(That's a joke. But for real. Just punch him a
little bit.)
Sincerely, Dany

I didn't want to send it because it sounded like a
robot wrote it. But if I sent nothing, then Zahira might
get sad. So I sent it, and I knew it wasn't enough, but
what else was I supposed to say? That they play
basketball on TV here? She doesn't even know I like
basketball. My heart feels empty about that. After
everything we went through, there's still so much we
don't know about each other.

How long has it been since I got here? Two months
in a coma. One month recovering. I'm still recovering. I
only just got strong enough to hold a pen last week, when
I wrote the letter. It was like I had to make my body
remember how to do everything. There's a physical
therapist who helps me with all that, and it's been
helping very, very slowly.

I have a mental therapist too, but that one's not
going so well. She just keeps trying to get me to talk about
what happened to Marisa. I don't even want to talk to
myself about Marisa. And she keeps saying everything
will be okay, blah blah blah. Yeah. I'm about to move
across the ocean to a whole different country with people
I don't really know, but sure. I'll be alright.

And she gave me a new diary. I threw it in the trash
the moment she left.

Well, Lilian fished it back out and now it lives on my

bedside table, but I haven't touched it. Even looking at it makes me all jittery on the inside, and I have to look away and think about literally anything else before panic crashes over me. I don't know. It feels like there's been a lot of that. A few months ago, any life I pictured with Marisa were gone, and there was nothing left. I was so sure I didn't have a future. I never pictured anything after Suddence.

And now, all of a sudden, I have all this time ahead of me, and it freaks me out. It makes my fingers all cold, and my ears start ringing and my heart wants to jump out of my chest and just book it. I still feel empty and wrong, and I miss Marisa so much but I can't think about her because it just makes me cry, and—and—am I supposed to live the rest of my life like this? Just wake up and feel bad and then go to sleep again?

Calm down, Dany.

I open Zahira's letter, and like I asked, there are about five pictures of Poquito inside.

Dear Dany,

I'm so glad to hear you're awake! And I'm glad to hear the hospital food doesn't suck. (And yes, I did punch Aaron on the arm, just like you asked.)

I hope you're doing good! I know being in the hospital isn't easy. I had to get surgery for my appendix when I was like, six, and all I really remember is that it was miserable. If I could, I would totally post some ice cream to your room, but I don't think the hospital would appreciate that :(

I hope you like the pictures of Poquito. Maybe one day you can come visit him for real. Then you can see that Shirley definitely doesn't have bald spots anymore.

I wish I could send you some pizza, too. The pizza here is surprisingly really good. Maybe next time I'll drip some pizza grease on the letter.

Get well soon!

-Zahira

I stare at the words *one day you can come visit*. She knows we're leaving. It's just wishful thinking.

Lilian comes back with a pen and a piece of lined paper. "What'd she say?" she asks.

I give her the letter and pick up the pen, but I don't know what to write. *I would love to come visit you! Unfortunately, we're leaving in a few weeks and it might be dangerous to see each other, so I'm going to pass. I don't believe that Shirley isn't bald anymore. Show me a picture and prove it.*

I end up poking my pen on the paper instead and eventually dig a hole through it.

Lilian glances up from Zahira's letter. "You alright?"

I stop poking and try to rub away the blot of ink I left on the plastic table. It smears and stains.

"When you…" I press my lips together, trying to put the question in the right order. "When Marisa called you, what did you guys talk about?"

Lilian looks surprised, and I know it's because it's the first I'm talking to her about Marisa. It's the first time I'm saying her name, period. Already, I can feel ice cold panic clawing at my heart, and I want to say *never mind* and do something else, but I take a deep breath and push the panic back.

Lilian has a faraway look in her eyes, and I realize maybe I'm not the only one who has trouble thinking about Marisa.

"In the beginning, we fought a lot," she says slowly, like she's sifting carefully through her memories. "I tried to get her to come back, and she was telling me how terrible my dad was, and I hated her for a while. The calls never went past a minute. I think she was afraid of being traced. But once it was clear she wasn't going to come back, we kind of...settled."

I try to imagine Marisa hiding in the motel washroom, calling Lilian when she thought I wouldn't notice. I picture anger, bitterness, fear. And sadness. My heart cramps.

"She talked about you, mostly."

I blink in surprise. "Me?"

"Yeah," she says with a smile, but I can't miss the tears in her eyes. "She talked about how you liked basketball, and musicals."

"It's just the one," I say a little defensively. It feels weird to be talking about Marisa like this, like she just left the room to get a snack instead of being gone forever. But it's nice, in some way. Like I've been trapping her for too long in my heart and now I'm finally letting some air in. It hurts, feeling like she might escape. But there's some relief, too.

"What about you?" I say. "What did you talk about?"

She sighs, and it seems to sag her whole body. "I don't know. I complained about the weather. I talked about visiting my family. Sometimes it felt like the good old days, when we were seventeen and the worst thing we had to care about was our finals. It was…" She turns away, wiping her eyes "It was nice. Being able to talk to her. Despite everything."

I stare down at the blank paper, my eyes blurring with tears, too. Quietly, I say, "I miss her."

I didn't realize how much I needed to say that until now. Something unlocks in my chest, and all the grief comes flooding out. I bury my face, trying not to cry, but it's impossible. I miss her. I miss Marisa. But she's never coming back.

Lilian puts a comforting hand on my back, and without thinking, I lean into her. She wraps her arms around me, and she feels warm and soft and safe.

"I miss her too," she says. "I miss her too."

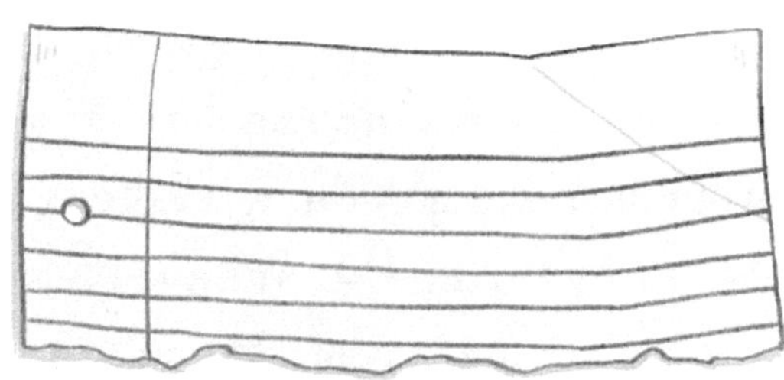

Dear Zahira,

I don't believe Shirley doesn't have bald spots anymore. Show me a picture and prove it.

You better not get that pizza oil on the letter. You'll invite a bunch of ants, and then you'll be blacklisted from sending letters for LIFE.

It's been nice and sunshiney here, which is great. I'm cold all the time now, so every time a patch of sun gets in my room, I sit under it like I'm one of those lizards in the pet store.

I've always wondered. You said you were a med student. Have you ever dissected a frog?

What about a cow? Have you ever seen a dead person? That's what I want to know.

I would love to visit Poquito. Marisa is allergic to fur, so we never had a pet. Once I found a rabbit caught in a raccoon trap at one of the motels, and I freed it and tried to sneak it into the room. It was there for about three seconds before Marisa started sneezing up a storm, and she told me to get rid of it. I let it go into the woods. I only had the rabbit for ten minutes, but I named it Goji.

There's a pizza store on the corner near the hospital. Maybe I can convince ~~Ma~~ Lilian to buy one for me, and I'll just pretend it's from your store. Yum!

Sincerely, Dany.

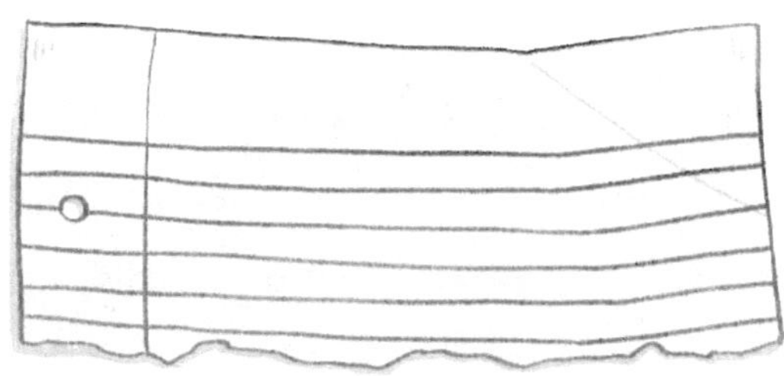

Dear diary.

Hi. I'm sorry I threw you in the trash and then ignored you for weeks. Looking at you still makes me feel all gouged up inside. But the fact of the matter is, I need somewhere to write. I have too many things in my head, and they need to go somewhere before I explode. And I looked to my right and oh! There you were. Like you're haunting me.

Let's start this off normal, okay? My name is Dany. I'm 11 years old. I had another diary before, but it got burnt to a bacon crisp in a high school. The funny thing is, I don't even remember when I lost it. Everything happened so fast.

Anyway. Getting to the point. Lilian told me a lot of things about Marisa and the clinic. And I keep turning it over in my head like those bingo balls and I feel like I need to write it all down before I forget. And I know you might be thinking, "Why would you even forget such an important thing?" Well, I can't help it, okay. My brain is still all groggy, like it got chopped up into little pieces. The doctor said the sepsis started destroying my organs and apparently I only had like a 15 percent survival rate or something. Yikes. So, yeah. I'm doing pretty well, considering All That.

So. Here goes.

I was born in Suddence. That one is true.

Marisa's parents died in Suddence. That part is also true.

Marisa joined Doctor Heed because of that. Also true.

New info: Marisa is the one who adopted me, but Doctor Heed and Lilian are also my legal guardians. Doctor Heed is legally my dad. This creeps me out.

And then there's just a bunch of things

Doctor Heed straight up lied about.

Marisa didn't suggest cutting me and the other kids apart. Nobody ever suggested that. The clinic's plan has always been to study us and train us.

It's true that Marisa ran away with me when she disagreed with the clinic. She agreed with them all this time, but when the day came to turn me in, she couldn't do it. She didn't run away to find somebody else to cut me up. She ran away to protect me.

You can see why I had to write all this down. Both of them lied. Both of them told the truth. What Lilian told me helped me realize which is which, but it all gets so tangled in my head. It's all just too much.

~~Sometimes I wonder if Marisa would still be alive if we believed Lilian from the start.~~

I think Marisa lied because she didn't think I would understand.

The worst part is, I think she was right.

ZAHIRA'S NEXT LETTER comes two weeks later. It has a picture of her posing in front of her pink truck, her arms outstretched towards it as if saying, *See?*

Dear Dany,

Oh, we dissected frogs, alright. And rats. And hearts. Almost everything. Our prof took us on a field trip to the funeral home once, and...yeah. There were definitely some dead bodies there.

So, I know you're probably leaving soon. I guess this will be my last letter. I'll miss you! And Shirley does NOT have bald spots. See for yourself.

I mean it, about you coming to visit. Maybe in a few years, when it's safe. You can come back and I can take you to the carnival. I bet you've never been on a roller coaster, huh? And then we can go to that arcade! They got even more claw machines. There's definitely a doll in there I've got my eyes on...

So. Time to get serious now. I've been trying to keep these letters fun and light. I didn't want to stress you out. But I have to say this before I don't have the chance anymore.

I know it seems like I slid back into my old life easily, but I just haven't been telling you the hard parts. It's been strange to just pretend like nothing ever happened. Sometimes I wake up and feel like I'm trapped in a glass bubble. I guess what I'm trying to say is: it'll be hard for you, too. Or, I guess, it's already been hard for you, all these months. But I just want you to know that it gets better. It won't be hard forever. I know trying to move on feels like trying to forget, and we don't want to forget. We don't want to let go.

But that's the thing. Moving on doesn't mean forgetting. One day, when you think about her, it won't hurt so much anymore. But that doesn't mean you're forgetting her, or leaving her behind. It means you learned how to carry her. And that's a good thing. I promise. Cross my heart and everything.

I hope you have a safe trip. I hope you

move somewhere with wonderful weather. And I hope Lilian lets you have a dog. Or a cat! Or possibly a rabbit for real. Here are some more pictures of Poquito to keep you company.

I'll miss you! Have a safe trip!

-Zahira.

I stare at the letter in a daze. I know she poured her heart into it, but all I can think is one thing.

I'm leaving soon.

This is it.

But there's still so much I want to say to her. I need to thank her. I need to apologize. I need more than a few hours hovering over a blank piece of paper, thinking and rethinking about what to write and then waiting days and weeks for a response. I need to see her. I need to talk to her.

But it's not possible. It's too risky. Lilian would never let me go. She did mention the possibility of a video call, but I've seen the other kids in my room do that with their family. The connection is always choppy and pixelly, and the sound is grating and tinny, and seeing Zahira like that as our last conversation would only make me feel worse. I just know it.

So write the letter, Dany. Just write the letter.

I ask for a pen and paper. I stare at the pale blue lines, my pen uncapped and ready to write. I should do what Zahira did, pour my heart into it, tell her how much I'll miss her before I don't have the chance anymore.

But all I put down is:

Dear Zahira,
Thank you for everything.

MY LETTER STAYS like that until the day comes for me to leave. A car is coming in the afternoon to take us to the airport.

I know I should write more. Even if I don't, I should at least put it in the mailbox. But instead, I just stuff it in my backpack and try to convince myself I'll come up with something profound and meaningful in the car.

But I have so much to say, and I don't know how to say them. I stare out the window, blankly watching the cars pulling in and out of the parking lot. I feel like I'm betraying her. After everything she did for me, I can't be bothered to write a stupid goodbye letter.

Lilian comes in with a packet of cheese crackers. "How're the clothes?"

"Fine," I say without turning away from the window, my chin still resting on my folded arms. I know it's rude and ungrateful. My new clothes fit me well, nice and breezy for the summery weather, and my new bag is clean and packed with everything from my old bag, along with my diary and a box of free hospital crayons and a cellphone for emergencies. I should be happy about leaving. Relieved, at least. I'm going somewhere safe. But dread is eating away at my heart.

So write the letter, Dany. That's the only thing holding you back.

But I feel stuck, and every second that passes on the clock only pulls panic closer to the surface.

God, Dany, just write the letter.

"Here." Lilian opens the cheese crackers and sets it on the window sill, but not before stealing one. "It's almost lunch. Do you want something from the hospital? Or I could get someone to buy something different."

"Like what?" I say listlessly.

"Hm. Well." Lilian peers out the window with me. "I see a sandwich place out there. Fast food. Or pizza?"

Pizza. Zahira works in a pizza shop. Not this one, though. She works in Metro Place, a mall in a city an hour away.

I watch a bus pull into a station beside the hospital, and an inkling of an idea seeps into my head.

I say, "Can I have ice cream and french fries?"

Lilian frowns. "For lunch?"

"It's…" I swallow my bubbling nerves. Be calm, Dany. Don't let her know what you're thinking. "Marisa, she, uh. She promised me one."

Her expression softens. "Okay, then. I'll get Harty to buy some for you."

Harty is one of the two guys who sit out in the parking lot, making sure Lilian and I are safe. Lilian steps outside the room to call him, and while she waits for him to pick up, I poke my head out and tell her I'm going to the washroom.

She nods, too distracted to notice I have my backpack on.

And she's too distracted to notice me slip past the washroom, heading for the stairs.

I speed-walk through the hospital, my heart galloping in fear. Any moment now, I'm expecting Lilian to burst out from the stairwell shouting my name, or Harty and his buddy to suddenly show up and herd me back to my room.

But the closer I get to the hospital entrance, the more excitement replaces the nervousness.

I'm almost there. And nobody is stopping me.

I hover by the big plants beside the automatic sliding doors, casing the world outside. I'm not exactly sure where Harty and his buddy are parked. I just know it's one of the blue cars, and I can't let them catch me.

My eyes go to the bus station. The bus I saw is already gone, but another one is sliding into place. A few people are already in line, and some people in the hospital lobby are getting up to catch the bus, too.

Perfect.

Following close behind a mother and her daughter, I slip out of the hospital and join the bus line.

IT TAKES MORE than an hour and one bus transfer to reach Metro Place Mall, and I'm wholly grateful for the bus drivers who smiled and explained how to get here. By the time I step off the bus, my head is already roiling over what I'm going to say when I see Zahira.

Surprise! I'd say, popping out from under the counter, and she'd be like, *What the hell are you doing here?* Would she be happy to see me? What if she gets mad and immediately sends me back to the hospital? What if this whole time she was secretly glad I'm disappearing from her life forever?

What if she isn't even here today?

Don't think about that, Dany. Just keep walking.

I cross the parking lot into the mall. It's the weekend, and the place is echoing with shoppers and music and screaming babies. When was the last time I went to a mall during normal hours? When was the last time I browsed the stores like a regular person?

I can't even remember. But I'm not here to browse

the stores.

After peeking at a map, I find my way to the food court. It's even more crowded than the rest of the mall, smelling of a thousand different types of food. I see a noodle place and a shawarma place and a juice spot. I spy a pizza shop, and for a second my chest lifts with excitement, but it isn't the only pizza place here. I see at least three more, and when I glance across the food court at the arcade, I realize all three are in perfect view of it.

I walk up to each store, scanning the workers and peeking into the kitchens to find Zahira, but she isn't here. She isn't in any of them.

I stumble back to the middle of the cafeteria, my head spinning. She has to be here. She *has* to. I turn in a circle, hoping to see a spot of pink, her mess of wavy hair. My eyes go back to the pizza stores, hoping she'll suddenly appear, but she isn't here. She isn't here, and I've made a huge mistake, and—

"Dany?"

I spin around. It takes a second to see her because she looks so different. Her hair is gathered in a tight bun, and she's wearing a collared shirt in the colours of the pizza store. She takes half a step towards me, eyebrows raised in surprise, and I'm already running across the cafeteria and throwing my arms around her.

"Dany," she says, still stunned, but she laughs and sinks to her knees to hug me. She's holding a lunch bag. She was just on her break, and I was panicking over nothing. "Dany, what...what are you doing here?" Then she pulls back, her expression concerned. "Where's Lilian? Did something happen?"

"No." I don't know when I started crying, just that suddenly my eyes are blurry and my voice is all wobbly. "Everything's fine. I just—" I pour back into her arms, squeezing her tight. "I had to see you. I couldn't just leave."

Zahira pats my back as I cry. "Does Lilian know you're here?"

I shake my head, still holding her tight.

"How did you even get here?"

"I took the bus," I say. "I used my special coins."

I can hear Zahira's frown when she says, "Special coins?"

I nod. Watching the ticket machines swallow the loonies and quarters, I felt a horrible pain in my chest, but it was worth it, because it's *this*. This is the reason I can't just leave. We went through all that together, and we don't even *know* each other. She doesn't know I like basketball. She doesn't know I collect special coins. I don't know her favourite colour. I don't even know her last name.

"Dany," Zahira starts.

"We could go." The words blurt out, and then I can't stop talking. "We could go. Right now. We could get on your truck and just drive away. We don't have to tell anyone where we're going. Just the two of us. We could just..." A sob catches my voice. "We could just go. We could stay together."

"Dany." She pulls away. "What are you talking about? I can't just leave."

"Yes, you can. You hate this job. You're miserable. We could escape."

She laughs, but there are tears in her eyes. "Thanks for thinking of me. But I'm okay here. Really. I'm getting back on my feet. I'll figure out a new future. And *you*." She gives me a little shake. "You have to go with Lilian. Remember? You promised me." Her face dips into mock seriousness. "Unless you were lying."

I don't know if I want to sob or laugh, and somehow end up doing both at the same time. "I didn't."

"Didn't what?"

"I didn't promise. You said *Got it?* and I didn't say anything."

She draws back, a smile crooking her lips. "It was implied."

I laugh and sob again, covering my face.

"Dany, hey. Come on." She pats my shoulder. "Really. What's wrong?"

I say, "Do you think we're friends?"

"Of course we are."

I can imagine her big eyebrows coming down as she says this, squishing into her eyes. I lower my hands and watch her, tears streaking both our faces. She means it. She really means it.

"I like basketball," I say. "I collect special coins. My favourite colour is green." I wipe my eyes. "What about you?"

"Me?"

I wipe my eyes again. "Friends have to know these things."

She drops her shoulders in a sigh, her lips twisting into a smile. "I play field hockey. I collect things that look like Poquito. And my favourite colour is..." She looks to the side for a moment, thinking. "Purple."

I frown even as I laugh. "Not pink?"

She shrugs. "I like them an equal amount."

"No, you have to have a favourite."

"Fine. Purple." She grins. "But pink is a close second."

We laugh, and she pulls me into a hug. I bury myself in it. This might be our last hug forever.

"I'll be okay," she says. "And you'll be okay. We'll promise each other, alright?"

I nod against her shoulder. "I promise."

"I promise."

We let go of each other, both of us wiping at our tears. And then we're laughing, and I don't know why.

Zahira sighs with a small, sad smile and says, "You have a way to contact Lilian? Tell her where to pick you up?"

"Yeah," I say. I pull out the emergency phone from the side pocket, but my fingers hover over the numbers. I look up at Zahira and say, "I'll miss you. And I'm sorry. About everything."

"In case you didn't notice, I forgave you a long time ago." She musses up my hair, and I giggle. God, when was the last time I giggled? "But thank you. And I'll miss you, too. Hey." She leans forward, like she has a secret to tell me. "After you call Lilian, she won't get here for, like, an hour. In the meantime, we could get pizza, and then we could…"

She jabs a thumb at the arcade, and I light up, nodding.

We do exactly that. I call Lilian, apologize for running away, explaining where to find me. Zahira treats me to a vegetable goat cheese pizza, which she swears is the best out of all of them. My mouth still salty from the pizza sauce, Zahira takes me through the arcade, scouting out all the machines we can cheat at. Skee-Ball. The coin pusher. Pinball. All the strange games that depend on luck more than skill to win the prizes inside, like positioning a scissor at the exact right place to cut a wire or making blocks of light stack up to reach the top of the screen. Some of them I can spark the prizes straight off their pegs, and some of them take me a while to get the hang of, but soon we're bundling prizes and long trails of tickets in our arms, reveling in our victory.

"Wait," I say when we pass the basketball game.

Zahira pulls back, a little out of breath from laughing. "This one?"

"We can race," I say, already slotting tokens in. "No cheating this time."

The feel of the basketball is familiar in my hands, and the temptation to spark the ball in the right path is just at the tips of my fingers, but I hold my sparks back. I let the balls fly in their own path. Only a few make it in, and I lose to Zahira big time, but I don't care because I'm laughing so hard my cheeks hurt, and I've never felt so happy.

Finally, we come to the claw machines. Zahira points to a doll that looks just like Poquito. She tries it once without my help, just to prove how rigged it is, and the moment nobody is looking, I spark the doll into the chute. Zahira squeals in delight, squeezing the doll to her chest.

We go through the machines one by one, collecting a prize from each, until Zahira's arms are too full for anything more. At the last machine, a white rabbit doll sits in the far corner, its red eyes twinkling.

"One more," I say, a little lightheaded from using my sparks. One last one.

The rabbit falls through the chute, and when I pull it out to show Zahira, she's looking out of the arcade. I turn to follow her gaze.

Lilian and Harty are standing near the cafeteria, scanning the mall with worried expressions. Lilian spots me and hurries over.

"Dany." She falls to her knees and smothers me in a quick hug. "Don't ever scare me like that again." She looks at Zahira and smiles, giving her a small nod. "We have to go now. Thank you, for watching over Dany." To me, she says, "Alright. Say your goodbyes. We have a plane to catch."

Slowly, I turn back to Zahira. There really is no more room in her arms, but I hold the rabbit towards her. "You can have this, too."

She blinks in surprise. "You don't want any of them?"

I stare down at the rabbit. "I don't know."

"You can keep that one. And…" She shifts the dolls around until she manages to pick one out. "Here. You can have Poquito, too."

"Really?"

"Really." After a moment of consideration, she shifts the dolls around again to reach into her pocket. She flicks out her pink, heart-shaped sunglasses and settles it on top of my head. "There. Those look way better on you."

I smile, and my eyes are blurring again. "Thank you." I hug her one last time, through the lumpy heap of dolls.

Thank you for everything.

"Have you ever had french fries with ice cream?" I ask.

"I have not," she says.

"It's good. I thought…if we had more time, we could have had some together. But maybe, if we pick a time, we can both eat it, and we can pretend we're eating it together."

"Good idea," she says. I can't see her face, but I can tell she's crying, just like me. "How about next Wednesday?"

"Next Wednesday," I agree. "For lunch." I pull away and hook a pinky finger around hers. "Promise?"

"Promise."

Sniffling back my tears, I smile. Lilian leads me away, and I give Zahira one last wave goodbye.

On the car, driving away from the mall, for the first time, I feel hopeful. I still have a hard time imagining a future, but for now, I can look forward to next Wednesday. It's a small start, but it's something, and one day, I'll be ready.

I hold Poquito and the rabbit tight. In the back of my mind, I name it Baklava.

I promised Zahira, but now, I promise myself, too.

I'll be okay.

Dear Zahira,
Thank you for everything.

Sincerely, Dany

ACKNOWLEDGEMENTS

Little did you know, *Suddence* is just a rip-off of the live action *Sonic the Hedgehog* movie.

Think about it. A weird kid with super sparkly abilities is all alone and sad after losing a parent figure? Check. The weird kid forcibly recruits an initially unwilling adult to drive them across the country? Check. There are nefarious forces after the kid? Check. The kid nearly dies in the end but is saved by the power of friendship? Check. Well, kind of. Heck, there was even going to be a scene where Dany is injured and has to be treated by an unqualified medical worker.

Alright, you caught me, I'm just joking. *Suddence* is not a rip-off of *Sonic*. I just get a nice sensible chuckle whenever I think of the similarities. *Suddence* actually started as a character design project in university. For years I didn't know what to do with it, until on a whim, I decided to combine it with another story idea, and bam! *Suddence* was born. It was originally going to be a novella, a sweet 40k words, just a nice little side project I can work on while I was too busy being frustrated with my main project, but somehow, it turned into a whole novel.

And it was a heck of a lot of work! So firstly, I want to thank my parents who, unbeknownst to the fact I was writing a book, allowed me to have the time and resources and support I needed in order to focus on finishing this book while I was briefly unemployed. (Seriously, I don't think I would have finished this book otherwise.)

Thank you to my dear critique readers: Victor Matthews, Frank DeCay, and Caroline Johnson, who pointed out all the weird plot things and one zillion typos.

Thank you to my friendos and test audience: Sarah Piironen, Sophia Fan, and Owen Twaites! I larb you guys.

Thank you to the peeps at Half Past Five, the very first people who saw my (unofficial) pitch for the story, who helped me hone my pitching skills. I figured out a lot of plot things while telling you about my little story!

Thank you to Calligraphr, the custom font website I used to create Dany's handwriting, and thank you to Annie Spratt and Marjan Blan on Unsplash, who provided the royalty-free photos I used for the paper textures.

And thank you to the fellow writers on The Queer Library server for providing moral support and answering my pressing questions, such as "what is the difference between reversing in automatic transmission and manual transmission" and "please help me figure out a cool pen name."

Lastly, thank you to my cats Milo and Mika, for being cute.

Thank you for reading my book! And thank you for reading the acknowledgements too. That's dedication.

ABOUT THE AUTHOR

Emily Welkin Chen is a Taiwanese-Canadian writer, illustrator, and animator. She spends too much of her day staring at the computer screen and curled up like a shrimp. She wears glasses, but you wouldn't know that because she always forgets to draw them in self portraits. She is afraid of worms.

You Are Now Entering Suddence is her debut novel.